# A FIRST EDITION FELONY

### An Emma Warwick Cozy Mystery
### Book 1

## AMELIA D. HAY

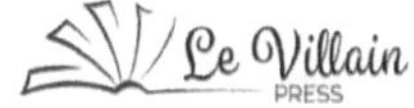

A First Edition Felony. An Emma Warwick Cozy Mystery, Book 1
Copyright © Amelia D. Hay (2025). All rights reserved.

www.ameliadhay.com

ISBN-13: 978-1-916609-06-8 (print)



Book cover design by Le Villain Book Covers at levillainbookcovers.com

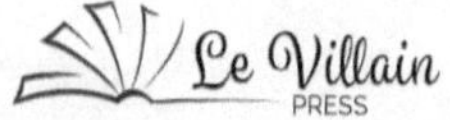

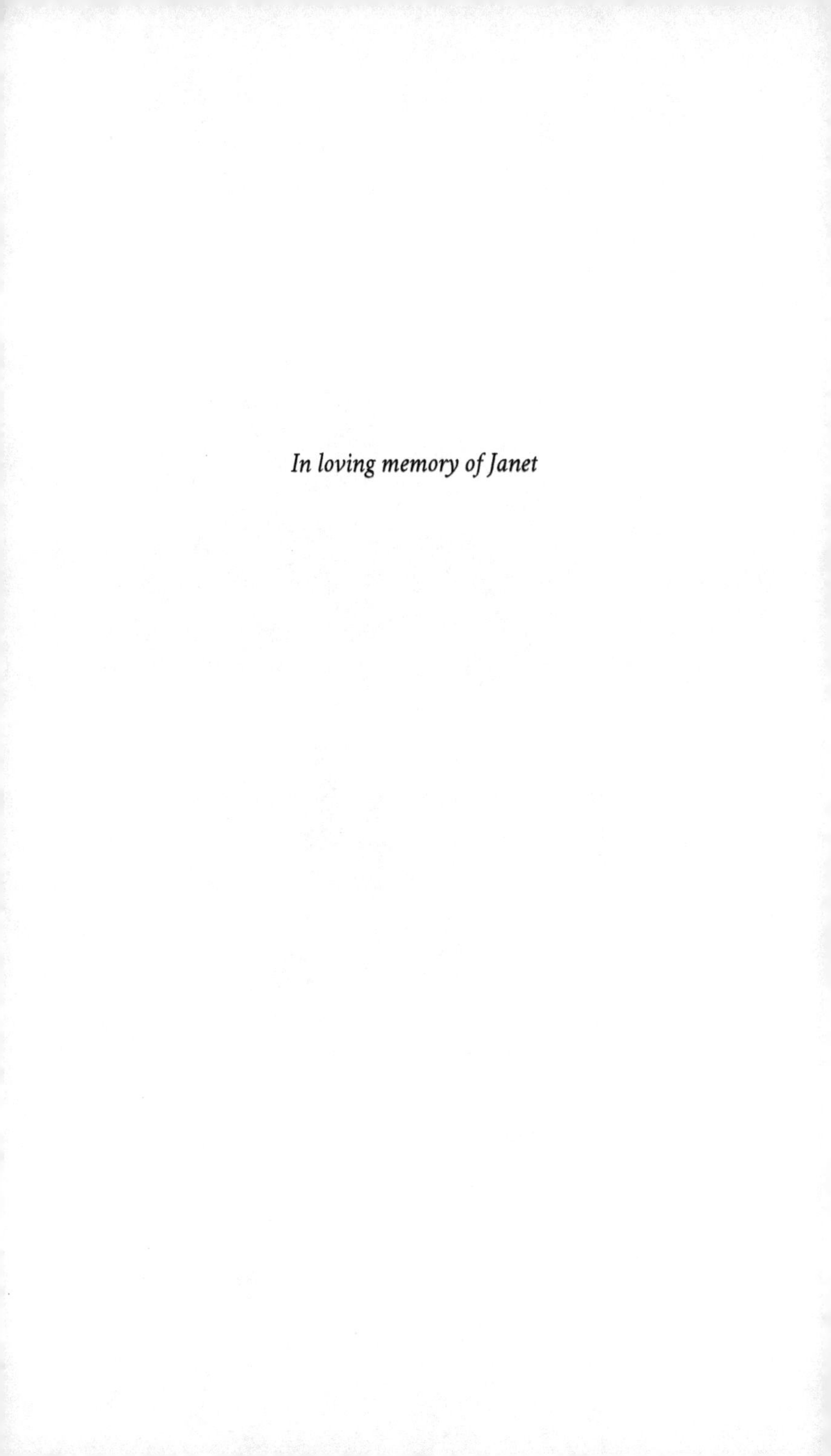
*In loving memory of Janet*

*"I have always imagined that Paradise will be a kind of library."*
*- Jorge Luis Borges*

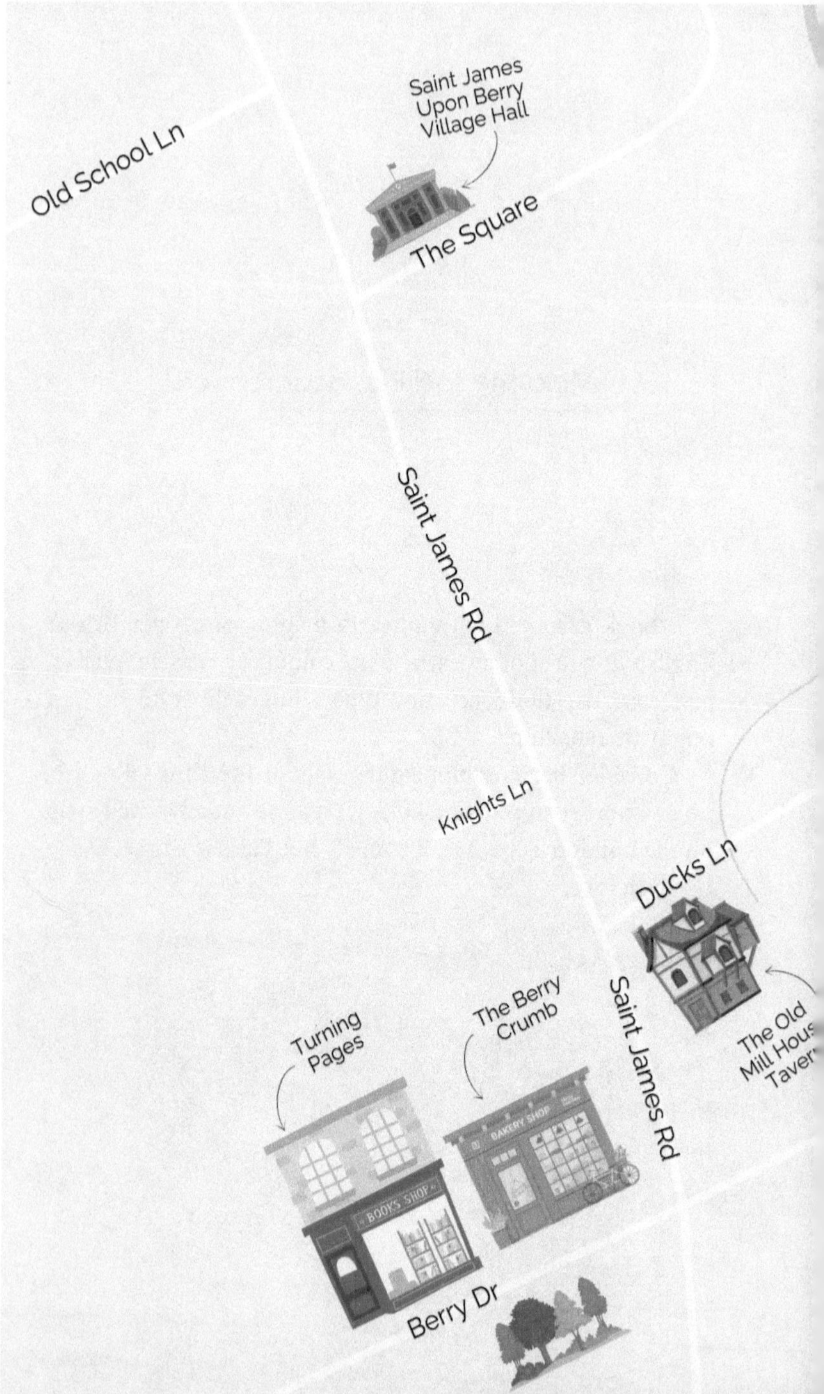

Old School Ln
Saint James
Upon Berry
Village Hall
The Square
Saint James Rd
Knights Ln
Ducks Ln
The Berry
Crumb
Turning
Pages
Saint James Rd
The Old
Mill Hous
Taver
BOOKS SHOP
BAKERY SHOP
Berry Dr

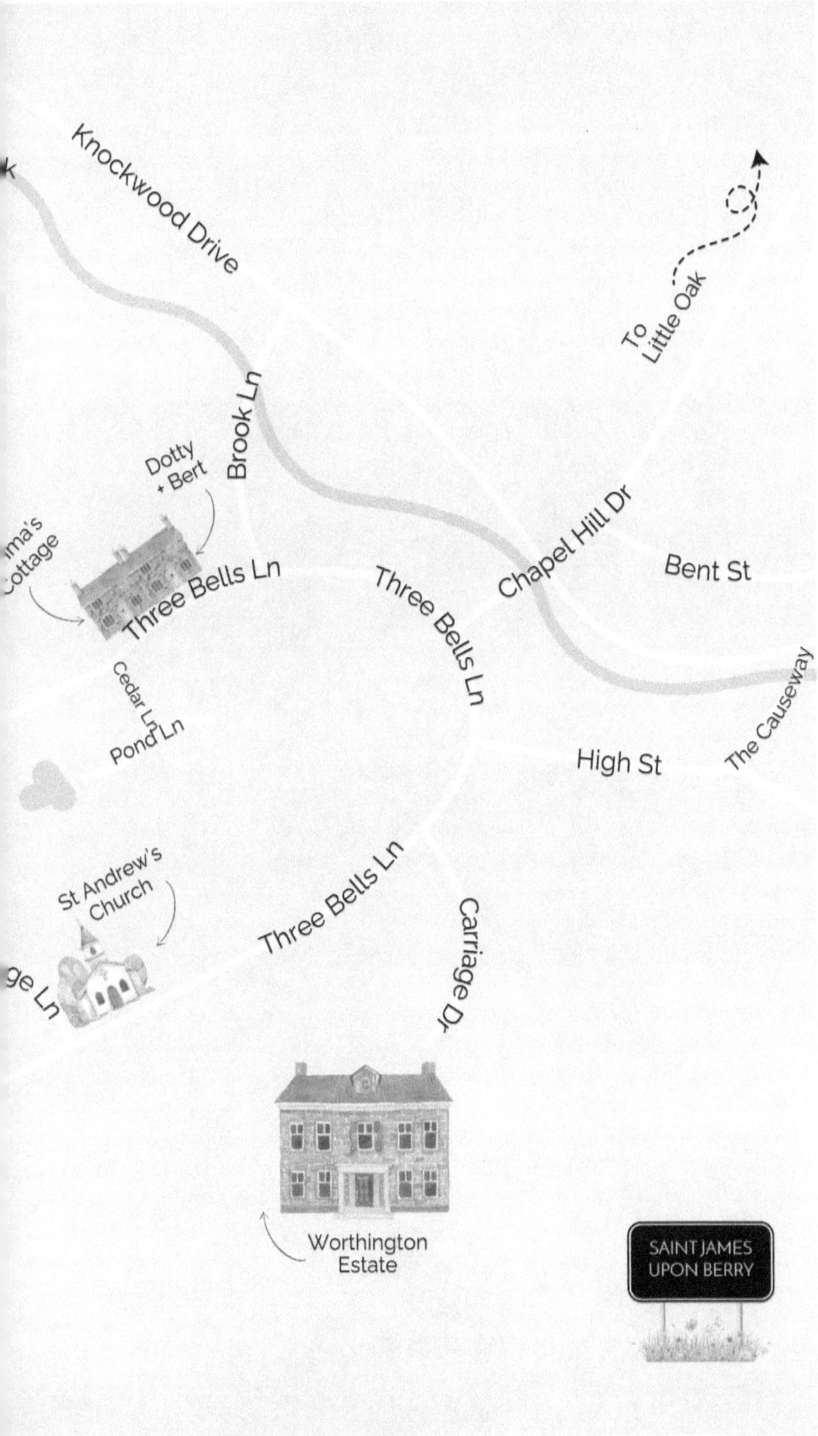

Knockwood Drive
Brook Ln
Dotty + Bert
Emma's Cottage
Three Bells Ln
Three Bells Ln
Three Bells Ln
Cedar Ln
Pond Ln
St Andrew's Church
ge Ln
Chapel Hill Dr
Bent St
To Little Oak
The Causeway
High St
Carriage Dr
Worthington Estate
SAINT JAMES UPON BERRY

## Chapter One

### THE WRONG END OF THE PINEAPPLE

*R*aindrops beaded down the windscreen as Emma Warwick drove along the idyllic narrow, winding hedge-lined laneways of the English village of Saint James Upon Berry in Hampshire. Vast fields of lush green grass whooshed by as she sailed down the road. The tiny town seemed out of place in the modern world. It was as if she had driven her electric vehicle into a bygone era. A digital *ding* chimed on the dashboard as she flirted with the wrong side of the speed limit. The windscreen wipers pivoted and swept away the rain, revealing the charcoal road and its leafy barrier. Ahead loomed a sky filled with grey clouds. Villagers of the sleepy town were probably peering out their windows and playing a little game of Spot the Londoner.

All Emma wanted to do was sleep in until two in the afternoon, hide from the world, eat chocolate, and binge another true crime docuseries on Netflix.

As embarrassing as it was to admit, three months ago, she had been let go from Byte Tech, the company she'd built from lines of code in her bedroom as a teenager. Byte Tech was the same company that her backstabbing tall, sexy geek of a husband—who seemed to only get better with age—had helped her build back when he was a brilliant programmer with kind eyes and empty pockets. But the public offering had changed him.

On the other hand, she was like wine, slowly turning into vinegar—sharp, cynical, and past her prime. There was nothing she could do about that. So if she was going to become vinegar, she might as well be balsamic—expensive, refined, and impossible to replace. The perfect revenge. A revenge body was far down on her to-do list, as evident by the tightening of her high-waisted jeans. But she doubted he would even notice, considering he had replaced her with that twentysomething leggy thing that he had hired as the head of Human Relations, who happened to worship the ground he walked upon.

The good news was that, hopefully, she would be free of that walking cliché in three months. As she recalled that fateful Sunday in October of the previous year, her heart raced, and her palms became clammy. She needed to calm down. Only three days into the new year and she was already stressed, anxious, and nauseated.

While the rest of the world recovered from a hangover, she had been invited to a secret board meeting with that man and the board of investors. With her lawyer by her side, she sat dumbfounded as she was kicked out of the company she'd created, offered a million-quid settlement, and on the way out, reminded of the yearlong noncompete clause in her contract. It was like repeatedly getting hit in the face by a fast-moving revolving door, and it had taken them only three months to stage this coup. He must have told the board the second she'd caught him cheating. What a sly fox.

A formulaic news-bulletin-inspired tune blasted through her car's speakers as a piece from Tchaikovsky ended. Classical FM was the only station not playing sappy love songs, so it was Classical FM or total silence.

'Coming up in today's news bulletin, Britons spent less this Christmas,' the announcer said.

'Yeah, Bill. It's no surprise, but Christmas sales from the previous year were down compared to the year before.'

Emma turned off the radio as she continued down the never-ending laneway. A sudden break in the hedges emerged. Out of nowhere was the world's smallest high street. It was a 'blink and you'd miss it' kind of moment. She brought her car to a crawl as she drove past the post office slash co-op supermarket. On the other corner was a bakery that claimed to be 'artisanal,' the Berry Crumb. She almost snorted as she read the sign—someone was a tad too optimistic about their baking skills. Sandwiched between those two shops was a bookshop called Turning Pages. The door to the shop opened. A tall, thin older woman with a pink-rinse pixie cut stepped out of the shop, a folded chalkboard sign under her arm. She pulled up the hood of her navy-blue raincoat with her free arm then waved as Emma headed towards Three Bells Lane.

Her hands trembled on the steering wheel. Seventy-two hours had passed since that New Year's Day boardroom ambush, and her body still hadn't recovered. That familiar ache throbbed within her as she peered out the window at the pink-haired woman outside the bookshop. Emma let her imagination run wild. The pink-haired woman was probably an independent bookshop owner, master of her destiny with no secret board meetings on holidays or corporate backstabbings dressed up as 'restructuring.' Knowing Emma's luck, Turning Pages was probably just another shop in a popular chain cleverly stamped with small-town charm.

The apparent simplicity of small-town business ownership beckoned like a forgotten dream. No complicated corporate structures or backstabbing boards—a far cry from the current state of her life. Amongst the dumpster fire that was her life, Emma had forgotten to reply to the estate agent and let them know that she would like them to look for another tenant for her quaint two-bedroom cottage purchased as an investment property before she married. Ten years ago, Emma had fallen in love with its charm and felt compelled to purchase it, her first major purchase as a rising tech CEO. Thankfully, she'd had the good sense to hire a lawyer and get a prenuptial agreement before she married that sly fox. At the time, hiring a lawyer for the prenup felt almost insulting to true love. It was the only decision from that era she didn't regret.

But thanks to her absent mind and the drama, the cottage was vacant, and she needed to do a walk-through and inspect her rental before they started looking for new tenants. That was the only reason she would drag herself out of bed in winter at thirteen minutes to six in the morning then take a two-and-a-half-hour drive to Hampshire. That Nora woman, or whatever her name was, had contacted her from the estate agent in the neighbouring village of Little Oak. She had insisted on a nine o'clock meeting at Emma's cottage and must be one of those crazy morning people.

Emma brought the vehicle to a stop as she reached the intersection of Berry Drive, the village's main road, and Saint James Road, which was almost perpendicular to Berry. Leaning over her steering wheel, she squinted at the street sign on the corner. It read Three Bells Lane.

Before her was more of the same: an idyllic narrow, winding, hedge-lined laneway with tall trees and vast green fields on either side. Holy crepes, someone had moved her grade II–listed, semidetached cottage. She leaned a little closer. The leather edge of her steering wheel dug into her sternum as she fought against the seat belt for a better view.

The sign read: Three Bells Lane. It was no hallucination—she was in the right spot. There can't be two streets named Three Bells Lane in the same village. That would be preposterous.

Emma peered at the empty streets. She tapped the screen of her smartphone in its cradle, navigated to the opposition's map app, and smiled. She selected the address for the cottage from a list instead of using her car's built-in navigation system. It wasn't user-friendly; it was as if the engineers had forgotten they were designing an app that would be used in a car. Apparently, having a PhD in computer science, twenty-four years of coding experience, and a successful IPO weren't enough for her to figure out how to use an in-built nav. Then again, she'd also failed to see the corporate coup coming, so maybe her skills had slipped over the years.

As the map slowly materialised on the screen, an unfamiliar whirring of an engine startled her. She glanced up into her rearview mirror. Two large tyres came into view. Perfect. She was holding up Old MacDonald in his red tractor.

The tractor driver tapped his horn as she leaned back, put her foot on the accelerator, drove across the intersection, and followed the long, picturesque, winding road.

———

Through the Old Mill House Tavern's foggy bay window, Emma watched droplets of rain race down the glass and puddle on the stone windowsill. It was half past eleven, and she had managed to empty a second pot of green tea in under twenty minutes. In the background, the ancient radiator crackled. At least that one worked. She groaned internally as she nursed the dainty blue-and-white teacup that reminded her of a vintage blue Asiatic pheasants pattern. Surely, a tavern in Hampshire wouldn't serve tea in an heirloom.

Surrounded by a sea of polished oak timber decor and

walls with antique-style lanterns mounted on them, she tapped the screen of her smartphone, and an image of the British Library loaded, the time overlaid in a pastel-blue font. For the fifteenth time, she checked to see if the handyman had called or sent a text. Nothing. She was hoping to hear an update. All she wanted was to leave Hampshire and return to London, but she was trapped in a tavern that was a nine-minute walk from her cottage.

Life had thrown a spanner into her plans, and she had to accept it one way or another. Emma had arrived to her appointment at her semidetached cottage one minute late to find Nora waiting. Quite naively, she'd thought the half-hour inspection would go swimmingly.

As she turned to walk out of the second bedroom on the upper level, the small radiator under the window caught her eye. It was missing a knob. So out of curiosity, like an idiot, she attempted to turn it on. The radiator groaned, spluttered, and rattled then went silent. Because it was winter, she couldn't put her two-bedroom cottage on the rental market until the heating was fixed. No one in their right mind would rent a property with a broken radiator. If she had simply let it be, she would have been back in London by now.

But things hadn't turned out like that.

Nora called the estate agent's contractor, and they waited. Ninety minutes later, the local handyman called and said the repair would have to wait until tomorrow. So, there Emma was thirty minutes later, having checked into the ninety-five-pounds-a-night double room, watching the rain fall down a bay window inside a dimly lit pub.

The little old lady behind the reception desk had beamed as she reassured Emma that the room would be available all week and she was more than welcome to stay as long as she liked. The more sceptical part of her brain—the part that had finally woken up three days too late—wouldn't be surprised if the owners of the Old Mill House were the elderly parents of the handyman she was desperately waiting to hear from, and it was all a clever ruse to boost the local economy.

She looked out at the desolate street corner of Saint James Road and Ducks Lane and stared at the beautiful green fields. Even in winter, the countryside was more stunning than ever, nothing but greenery and tranquillity. Time seemed to stand still, untouched by corporate takeovers and betrayals. Perhaps that was exactly what she needed. Why was she in such a hurry to do the inspection and return to London? All that awaited her was a tiny two-bedroom flat and LinkedIn notifications she couldn't bear to read.

Outside, a woman and a small child dressed in matching yellow raincoats hurried past, huddled over in the January chill. Both cast curious glances at the pub's only patron. Before Emma could get up, a tall, slender figure in Wellington boots, jeans, and a navy hooded raincoat dashed to the door. With a loud *creak* and the jingling of a tiny bell, the door to the tavern swung open, bringing in with it a gust of damp air that left a chilly bite and the woman with the pink-rinse pixie cut she'd seen earlier outside the Turning Pages bookshop. As she approached the Tavern's counter, she reached into her left raincoat pocket, pulled out a pile of loose coins and frantically counted each coin. Poking out of her right pocket was the edge of a white-and-red tube that reminded Emma of a popular brand of toothpaste. It was nice to see that she wasn't the only person who brushed her teeth at work.

If Emma was stranded there all day, she might as well visit the only bookshop in the village and purchase a birthday gift for her mother. At least one person should get something they wanted this year.

# Chapter Two

## A NOVEL PREDICAMENT

The smell of freshly cut grass with a note of cucumber and a dash of a delicate perfume-like aroma lured Emma away from the black-framed, glass-panelled double doors to the left of the large bay window of the Victorian shopfront at Turning Pages. Its large leftmost window was jam-packed with face-out editions of titles from bygone eras. Under the window was a large flower box filled with in-bloom white pansies and true-blue violas. She ran her finger along their wet petals. The flowers were real. Who knew flowers could bloom in winter?

Emma always marvelled at people who could grow things in general. All she managed to do was kill plants: a potted rosebush, two succulents, and one cactus. Yes, that was right. She'd killed a cactus. Maybe she should've read the instructions on the tiny card before throwing it away.

In what Emma thought was a spark of brilliance, she decided to walk from the Old Mill House Tavern to Turning Pages. Her great idea soon turned out to be a disaster. The fifteen-minute walk was up a slope, and her shins had paid a high price. Not only that, but her feet were killing her because the knee-high winter boots she wore over her dark denim jeans were not made for walking. But they were beautiful.

A light winter breeze blew back the hood of her stone-coloured rain parka, exposing her long dark-brown hair, which was tied up in a high ponytail. The ends of her hair formed soft natural waves and fell into the hood. Cold rain droplets beat down on her head as she leaned forward to inspect the covers on display in the shop window. She shivered as the wind blew through her open rain parka and cream woollen turtleneck sweater with thin horizontal navy stripes. It was her favourite jumper because it hid her disastrous midsection.

The black sign with gold lettering hung from two chains from a short post above the front door and jingled in the wind as if the store were begging her to enter. Pulling up the hood of her parka, she waltzed to the door and peered over at the chalkboard A-frame sign that simply read Rare Books Inside. Maybe she would find a gift for her mother after all.

*Ding, ding.* The tiny brass bell over the door to Turning Pages rang as Emma stepped inside. While holding the door open, she slipped off her coat and shook the rain off outside. After closing the door behind her, she hung her parka on the rustic solid-oak coatrack behind the front door. Inside the shop, it was cold—a winter chill clung in the air. Someone had left the door open for too long, and the shop's radiators were struggling.

A voice called out from somewhere in the depths of the bookshop, 'Just a moment.'

Emma wandered into the store, up the three steps between the entry and the main floor, and gazed around its beautiful interior. As far as the eye could see, floor-to-ceiling rustic oak bookshelves spanned the room's perimeter and slightly shorter bookshelves of the same material in the centre, each laden with books. The shelves acted as a maze.

It was almost alluring. Something magical compelled her to walk and get lost in a literary world. If she were honest, she couldn't remember the last time she had sat down with a novel and got lost in another world. Byte Tech had taken over her life, and she had little to show for it. Her CEO position had left her with zero free time.

An antique cash register sat on a counter made of the same wood as the shelves and coatrack. The counter was plonked down next to the newel post of the handrail of the small steps. Behind that were bookshelves bearing bookish knickknacks and books with ivory cardboard bookmarks poking out between the pages. Beside the counter was a white three-tiered rolling library cart that was surprisingly empty. The floorboards creaked as she wandered past.

As she meandered through the literary maze, her eye caught an expensive-looking navy scarf hanging over a rung of a wooden rolling library ladder along the shop's back wall. As she followed the bookshelves to the far-right wall of the shop, she spotted a collection of antique-style books sitting on a shelf next to an old Remington Model I typewriter. Obviously, those weren't real.

Emma ambled down the next narrow passageway of bookshelves towards the counter and stared at a pile of books under it. Along their spines were the words *Die Trying*. In an obnoxiously large font was the name Harry G. Evans. Someone had quite the ego—the author's name was bigger than the title. That name must be a pseudonym.

She strolled into the second half of the shop and peered down a short, narrow passageway lined with books before it came to a dead end. Nestled in the corner, in front of the shelves, was a massive teal-green beanbag. Three large ivory pillows were propped against the bookshelves, creating a makeshift reading nook.

The doorbell at the front of the shop jangled as the door slammed shut.

'Elsie, I'm in the back,' a soft female voice called out from the depths of the shop.

Footsteps thumped along the polished floorboards, getting harder and louder with every stride. Someone was headed towards her. So there were two customers and no actual staff. The lack of staff confirmed that those antiques weren't authentic. Maybe Emma could find a special edition of *The Great Gatsby* for her mother. Or was it *Tender is the Night* that her mother loved?

Emma reached for the side pocket of her parka. She froze. Holy crepes. She'd left her smartphone in her parka on the coatrack at the front of the store. Someone should change that chalkboard sign to read 'Free tech inside—help yourself.'

Whirling around, Emma dashed towards the front of the store. As she reached the end of the narrow bookshelf passageway, she collided with the pink-rinse lady she had seen earlier in the morning. Emma staggered back and hit her head against the side of the wooden bookshelf behind her.

'Are you okay?' The woman smiled. 'These bookshelves are known to have treacherous blind spots. I'm Elsie Reed, by the way.'

Emma nodded, unsure how to respond to the polite hazard warning.

A look of recognition swept across her face. 'I know you.' Elsie pointed at Emma. 'You're the electric-car lady from this morning. You know, that car is very quiet. It's pretty surprising. You could run over someone unsuspecting with that car.'

Emma shrugged. 'Like my ex-husband.'

'Mine too. Maybe we could line them up outside.' Elsie leaned in conspiratorially.

'Maybe not in broad daylight.' Emma nodded towards the front of the store.

Elsie chuckled. 'Don't worry. The villagers won't tell a soul.'

Emma raised her eyebrows.

'I take it you've been left to wander Turning Pages all on your own?' Elsie rolled her eyes.

Emma shrugged. 'Look, I don't want to get anyone in trouble.'

'Rubbish.' Elsie waved dismissively.

'So, is this your shop?'

'Oh yes.' Elsie beamed. 'It's been mine for the last ten years. You know, I used to be the editor for the crime author Charles Thomas Worthington the Third. So I can get you a few signed copies if you like at no extra cost.' Elsie gestured at the shelves around them and beamed. 'When I retired, I opened this shop. Sometimes, you have to create your own opportunities.'

Emma felt an immediate kinship with this woman who'd built something from nothing. It reminded her of those early days as a teenager coding the software for Byte Tech in her childhood bedroom, when anything seemed possible and her future was bright.

Elsie nodded over her shoulder, turned around, marched towards the counter, took a sharp left, and stood opposite the shelves closest to the register. 'This wall here is all signed copies, and in the corner are rare books.'

Emma nodded, pulled a novel off the shelf, and flipped through it. 'I've never read that much crime fiction.'

'It's not too late to start.'

She closed the novel and slipped it back on the shelf. 'Did you work for one of the big publishing houses?'

'Oh no.' Elsie's eyes sparkled with that familiar entrepreneurial fire that had once burned inside her. 'Charles thought he was getting a raw deal, so he took his literary agent, Richard Mortimer, and formed a publishing house. It's called Cloak and Dagger. And Richard formed a literary agency too.'

Emma grimaced. 'Cloak and Dagger? Isn't that a little too on the nose?'

Her words hung in the air, sharp and irretrievable. There she was criticising names with a woman who called her shop Turning Pages. At that point, Emma was opening her mouth only to change feet.

The narrow little bookshelf corridor grew quiet. 'You mean, like Turning Pages?'

'Yep,' Emma said in a surprisingly high-pitched tone.

Thankfully, from the back of the store, a series of loud crashes saved Emma from further humiliation. Without hesitating, Elsie sprinted off, weaving in and out through the maze of books. Emma followed, rasping as she struggled to keep up with the older woman. The bookshop owner was at least twenty years older, but she was way fitter. Maybe Emma could spend some of her newfound free time working out. The mere thought of that sounded excruciating.

Elsie gasped as they turned the last corner. At the other end of the room was an open doorframe that seemed to lead to a stockroom. In front of that open door, a young woman was on her knees, hunched over a pile of books.

'Noelle, are you okay?'

The teary-eyed woman with dyed fire-engine-red hair with dark-brown roots peered up at them. 'No bones, just my pride.' She smiled, and her high cheekbones and bright-blue eyes seemed almost out of place, like they belonged on a different face.

'Let me help you.' Elsie dashed down the end of the corridor and crouched.

'It's fine.' Noelle shrugged. 'I can do this.'

Elsie got up and sauntered down the narrow passageway towards Emma. 'Actually, quite conveniently, this is the crime section.' Elsie sighed. 'You don't like crime, do you?'

Emma tossed her head from side to side. 'Well, it's my mother's birthday coming up towards the end of January, and I wanted to get her a special edition of *The Great Gatsby* or *Tender is the Night*.' Emma paused as she tugged at the hem of her woollen turtleneck sweater. 'I want to get her a collector's item.'

In the background, Noelle's head bobbed up at the mention of the book titles.

Elsie nodded. 'It depends on how much you want to spend. I have some lovely new limited editions with colour pages and an edition from 1996.' She leaned in. 'It's a bit pricy. And a rare UK first edition that you'll need to take a mortgage out on to purchase. You know, it's one of three thousand copies.'

Together, they weaved through the maze of books and returned to the front of the store. They turned right and ambled past the ladder. Elsie shook her head at the navy scarf.

Elsie pointed at the Remington Model 1 typewriter. 'This is a typewriter similar to one that Charles Thomas Worthington the Third still uses, the one he's used to write all of his one hundred and fifty books, including those written under his not-so-secret pen name.'

'Is he a famous local author?'

Elsie raised her eyebrows. 'You've never heard of him before? His books frequently populate the bestseller charts.'

'Sorry. I have no clue.'

Elsie smiled. 'Well, you've heard of him now.'

She turned and ran her finger along the spines of the books. Upon reaching the last book on the shelf, she froze. Next, Elsie examined the shelves below and above the book.

'How expensive is this novel?' Emma asked as a boulder-sized rock formed in the pit of her stomach.

Elsie turned. Her face was pale, like a sheet of blank printing paper fresh from its packet. 'Oh, it's just ninety-nine thousand pounds and change.'

So, those books were rare limited editions, and they were sitting out in the open for all to see and touch. Judging by the expression on Elsie's face, one was missing. Maybe it was in the stockroom.

'It's missing.' Elsie's eyes glazed over. 'I know what you must be thinking. Who puts rare editions out on display?' Elsie sighed. 'We pack them up every night and put them out the next morning. And we're always in the store during the day.' Elsie dashed along the narrow space to the back left-hand corner of the store.

# Chapter Three

READING THE ROOM

A few minutes later, Emma wheezed as she dashed after Elsie through the maze of bookshelves, dodging a rolling ladder near the corner of the front-left bay window and the left-side wall. After almost colliding with a stack of paperbacks on the floor, propped up against three empty shelves, Emma turned the corner and followed Elsie through the literary labyrinth. The last thing Emma needed was to be known as the woman who'd damaged their stock.

Five minutes later, Elsie emerged from the backroom. The missing first edition didn't appear to be in the stockroom, but Emma didn't know for certain. Judging purely based on Elsie's sharp intake of breath and trembling hands, someone had stolen something expensive. Fingers crossed, it wasn't the ninety-nine-thousand-quid edition of *The Great Gatsby*.

'But I would've sworn it was here this morning,' Elsie muttered to herself. 'When did I last see it? Was it there when we packed up last night?' She squeezed past Emma and ran through the maze. Whirling around, Emma followed after her, continuing to wheeze. Emma was embarrassingly unfit.

Elsie paused as she reached the far right-hand corner of the shop, where the rare books were housed. Out of nowhere, Noelle slipped past Emma in the narrow shop aisle, stood next to Elsie, and peered up at her. Noelle brushed her hands along her black trousers then smoothed down the edges of her apron branded with the shop's logo. Her eyes darted between the shelf and Elsie.

'I swear I saw it this morning. I helped you set them up, remember.' Noelle nudged Elsie.

'Yeah'—Elsie ran her fingers along the spines—'but I can't be certain. Maybe it wasn't.'

Then Elsie froze. 'The *Gatsby* is gone.' Elsie gasped. It was as if she didn't believe the words coming from her mouth. Her shoulders fell as she slumped forward. 'I'll have to ask you to be a witness for insurance purposes. I hope you don't mind.' Elsie sobbed. 'And I'll have to talk to the police. This is so embarrassing.'

'Don't worry. I'll help you,' Emma said as she watched the two women in front of her. 'When was your last sale?'

Noelle cocked her head and rolled her eyes.

'Actually'—Emma glared at Noelle—'it's always best to start with the figures. They never lie. Your last sale should tell you who was at the till, when, and what they purchased. So—'

'It should tell me who was last in the store,' Elsie said, reading her train of thought. 'You see, we have a loyalty system where the customer gets ten pounds off their next order after their tenth stamp.'

'And that antique can tell you that?' Emma pointed at the golden antique cash register on the rustic oak counter.

Elsie turned and nodded to the side, gesturing for Emma to follow. Then, she dashed down the aisle to her left, along the right-side wall to the counter, with Emma following closely.

'No, we have a proper cash register underneath the counter,' Elsie said over her shoulder.

*Click.* Elsie opened the swinging side door to the checkout counter then pulled out a hideaway computer desk made from the same polished wood. Sliding out a screen no bigger than a tablet with a matching black stand, Elsie sighed. A short time later, Noelle emerged from the bookshelf stacks, clutching her smartphone to her chest.

Elsie swallowed hard as she stared at the screen. 'Our last client was Dotty Bennett. There's no way she stole *The Great Gatsby*. She was here this morning. She's a little old lady, and she purchased *Yesterday's Problem* in preparation for Charles Thomas Worthington the Third's book launch signing at Little Oak's Leaf & Leather.' Elsie sobbed. 'If I don't get this book back, I'm done. As it is, I'm already struggling to make rent. I've made a massive mistake, and I'm about to lose everything.'

The words hit Emma like the final knockout punch in a boxing match. She knew exactly what it was like to have a dream threatened as a result of poor judgment. Just months ago, she'd lost Byte Tech in a similar blindside. As she cast her mind over the last few months before that fateful day in October, she remembered her similar mistakes, the red flags she'd willingly ignored, all because she'd trusted someone.

Rain beat down on the front windows as lightning crackled. Outside, the sky had transformed into a darker shade of grey. The clouds showed no signs of shifting. The walk back to the Old Mill House Tavern loomed ahead, a soggy prospect.

Noelle wandered from the bookshelves to the checkout counter. A hint of satisfaction flickered in her eyes as she peered at Emma as if she was saying 'I told you so.' But to her credit, she was smart enough not to smile outwardly. Her pleasure at the discovery seemed peculiar.

'Wait.' Emma grimaced. 'But you were Charles's editor. Why isn't he doing book signings in your store instead of at this Leaf & Leather place?'

'He's a viscount.' Elsie blushed. 'I can't just ask him to do a book signing here.' She shrugged. 'I wouldn't want to make him feel like he owes me anything.'

Emma leaned back. 'Why not? You have a great industry connection and a personal relationship with the man. And your store could do with the publicity. It's midday, and you're empty.'

'Maybe.' Elsie glanced around the store.

'But back to your last customer. Maybe you could ask her a few questions about what she saw in the store this morning. There might have been another customer in the store who didn't purchase anything.' Emma shrugged.

Elsie's eyes bulged. 'No way. I can't interrogate my clients. Besides...' Elsie leaned over the counter. 'Dotty is the village gossip. The entire village will know in thirty seconds.'

Noelle's smartphone let out a digital church-bell-like chime. She jumped, nearly dropping the device, then scurried towards the stockroom. 'I need to take this,' she said over her shoulder.

'That's okay.' Emma nodded then asked Elsie, 'What about security? Do you have a video surveillance system?'

The shop manager slumped forward, resting her elbows on the counter and her head in her hands. 'I don't have security cameras. I can't afford it.'

Emma paused then took a deep breath. A part of her wanted to leave Byte Tech where it belonged, but she had to help the woman. 'My... former company, Byte Tech Inc., has a cheap surveillance software package that works well with an affordable three-camera system. You can get it for one hundred pounds.' Emma leaned in towards Elsie. 'I can show you a hack to make it work with the system. My rental property has radiator issues, so I'm at the mercy of the local handyman. I'll be in town for a while, so I may as well be doing something.'

'You don't have to do that.'

'Codswallop. It won't be too much of a faff.' Emma waved. 'And technically, I'm getting my techie revenge. One camera system at a time.'

'I'm screwed.' Elsie gasped, placed her hand over her mouth, and sat on the dark-brown leather armchair with rounded arms and an arched high back, which was pushed to the side behind the counter. 'There's a wealthy antique collector by the name of George Harrington. Technically, he's a Lord or something like that. He's expressed interest in the *Gatsby* and is bringing a specialist around tomorrow. He's expecting me to close the store and everything.'

'And he's a local?'

'Yes.' Elsie's face turned pale. 'I needed to make this sale for the cash flow.' Elsie gestured to the bookshelves. 'I know this is going to sound silly, but this bookshop was my dream, and it's slowly going under.'

Emma slipped her hands inside her jeans pockets and smiled sympathetically. It wasn't a silly dream. She knew what it was like to have a dream slip away, thanks to recent events. After all, she'd named Byte Tech and written those first few lines of code that sly fox had immediately recognised as 'pure genius.' But no one was on her side when everything went belly-up. The board was like a private men's club from the Regency era—no women allowed. Maybe she could help change things for Elsie. She saw no reason that poor Elsie should suffer the same fate. Not on Emma's watch.

'It's not silly.' Emma smiled. 'Let me help you. Order the cameras, and I'll send you a link to the software. You can order them from the place named after that river.' Emma picked up a business card off the edge of the counter in front of the antique cash register. 'I'll send you the link. If you order it today, it'll arrive tomorrow. I'll help you install it.'

Elsie tossed her head in a side-to-side motion. 'I can't afford it.'

'You just lost ninety-nine thousand pounds,' Emma whispered. 'What if they come back for more?'

A look of horror swept across Elsie's face. 'Okay.' Elsie sighed. 'I'll buy the security system.'

'It won't be that expensive.' Emma gave her a sympathetic smile. 'I'm pretty sure I can do it on a shoestring budget, but hopefully, you'll get it back.'

Something strange was going on in that shop. How could someone walk out undetected with a rare first edition? Did they get help? Or did they get lucky and turn up at the store at the right time while Elsie and Noelle were busy elsewhere? And what was with Noelle's odd behaviour? A piece of the puzzle was missing, and Emma was determined to find it. It was gnawing at her.

## Chapter Four

BREWING SUSPICIONS

*R*ain plummeted down against the front bay windows of Turning Pages. It was official—Emma was trapped and forced to wait out the rain in the bookshop. Technically, that wasn't an actual problem; after all, she was trapped in a literary haven on a weekday and with a huge settlement on its way to her bank account.

'You should check out the Berry Crumb. It's next door,' Noelle called out from behind. 'Ben is quite the dish, and so are his pastries.'

Emma peered over her shoulder at Noelle. A faint pink crept into Noelle's cheeks as she talked about Ben. She raised her eyebrows. 'I've sworn off all men.'

'Of course you have.' Noelle's gaze flicked upwards. 'Well, be prepared. Ben will make you see the light.'

Emma stood at the door and peered through the large window at the desolate grey streets. On the opposite side of the narrow laneway of Berry Drive was a hedge barrier. Behind that were tall trees and vast green fields that stretched as far as the eye could see. A patchwork of shades of grey loomed in the background.

A churning noise cried out from the depths of her stomach, disturbing the silence of the sleepy bookshop. Maybe the Berry Crumb wasn't the worst idea. But she wasn't going for a man, no matter how much of a dish he seemed. Emma was hungry.

She grabbed her rain parka off the rustic oak coatrack and put it on. Perhaps out of habit and years of living in London, Emma patted the front pockets of her parka in a desperate search for her smartphone. Her hands brushed against a long rectangular object. She slipped out her phone, woke it from sleep mode, and navigated to a shopping app.

With a few quick clicks, she located the cameras in the online store and copied them into a text using the handy 'send this to a friend' link. Holding the business card in her left-hand, Emma used her right thumb to type Elsie's mobile phone number into the 'to' section at the top of the screen.

In the background, Noelle wandered around, and her shoes clacked against the polished wooden floors. Hairs on the back of Emma's neck stood to attention. The young woman was hanging around for a reason. Emma could feel her presence. Maybe Noelle was just curious about the message Emma was sending, but one thing was certain: she was being watched.

After zipping up her coat, Emma pulled up the hood and pushed the front door open, triggering the jingling of the brass bell. Stooped forward, she dashed out the door, clutching her hood. Rain dripped down her arm, soaking the cuff of her woollen turtleneck sweater as she crept along the side of the building. As she reached the edge of the second bay window, the raindrops ceased. She had arrived at the covered entrance to the Berry Crumb.

A brass bell chimed overhead as Emma pushed open the single front door of the Victorian-style shop. Letting the door close behind her, she surveyed the bakery.

'Welcome to the Berry Crumb. I'm Ben,' a male voice called out from somewhere within the depths of the shop, above the sound of the rain hitting the window.

In front of her was a long glass counter that spanned two-thirds of the shop's length. The final third was occupied by a cash register and a lift-up counter, allowing staff access to the behind-the-counter area. The counter closest to the right wall was filled with baguette-style sandwiches with cheese, lettuce, tomato, and various meats bulging out the sides. Next to the sandwiches, filling the majority of the space within the glass counter, were a variety of pastries, tarts, sweet breads, and two cakes. Behind the counter were shelves of bread and a professional coffee machine.

'Dear, you won't catch me going out in that weather,' a feminine voice said from behind her.

Emma turned. Sitting in the right bay window, on a light-blue gingham-checked cushion at a table for six, was a petite elderly woman whose short straight hairstyle with a side-swept fringe reminded Emma of Julie Andrews, apart from the blue rinse. She was dressed all in black: tunic, tights, and small patent leather ballet flats. Each item of clothing seemed to be the same shade. Hunched over an unfinished baguette with an open navy puffy coat with a fur-trim edge reminis-cent of a sleeping bag, she smiled. On the right-hand side of her plate was a white teapot and matching teacup and saucer.

'Get the ham-cheese-and-tomato baguette.' She placed her hand on her chest. 'Honestly, I'd sell my Bert in a heart-beat for the last piece.' The little old lady leaned in conspira-torially. 'Just between you and me, I'd recommend skipping the toasting. Ben struggles with the toaster. He's more of a pastry chef and less of a regular cook. One day, I watched him blow up a microwave.'

'Dotty,' a male voice said with a chuckle.

After turning around, Emma waved at the tall, thin man

with dirty-blond hair and almond-shaped green eyes. He smiled. And that was when she saw him flash a set of perfectly straight white teeth. The man seemed more like a movie-star than a small-town pastry chef. And he was skinny. Can you really trust a thin pastry chef?

'It's lunchtime, so you can't go wrong with the ham-cheese-and-tomato baguette. They'll sell out fast,' he said.

Emma narrowed her eyes, glanced at the four ham-and-cheese baguettes, then peered over her shoulder at the pouring rain and empty streets.

He chuckled. 'Saint James Upon Berry might be a small town, but we have DishNDash.'

Emma nodded.

'There's only one left.' Ben leaned over the counter and winked.

Emma raised her eyebrows at him. 'You can turn it off, mister. I'm stranded here.' She pointed over her shoulder.

'So, are you new in town?' Ben bit the inside of his lip.

It was official—she was running out of bandwidth, and to get a bite to eat, she had to flirt with that soppy lush behind the counter. No wonder little Miss Twentysome-thing Potential Book Thief had been impressed. Then it dawned on her. She knew exactly how to get rid of the man.

'Yeah, I'm middle-aged, separated, and going through a high-profile divorce.' Emma peered across the room at Ben, who had grabbed a pair of obnoxiously long tongs and tossed them in the air.

Ben chuckled. 'Okay, I can take a hint.'

Emma stifled a laugh. 'Can you, though?'

Ben turned a dark shade of crimson as he dropped the tongs on the floor.

Emma approached the counter and wandered down to the baguette section. 'I'll have the ham-cheese-and-tomato baguette, a pot of green tea, and a bottle of still water.' She pointed at the refrigerator behind the baguette counter.

'Jasmine, matcha, or sencha?'

Emma raised her eyebrows. 'Jasmine.'

Ben nodded as he sauntered to the cash register, punched in her order, stared at the screen, glanced up at her, and flashed that same alluring smile. The man certainly had charisma, almost too much for his own good.

'That'll be fourteen seventy-five. Cash or card?'

That was why he was so flirty. He charged London prices in a small village. Fine, two could play that game. She pulled out her husband's black Amex, which he'd forgotten to cancel, and slapped it on the counter.

Ben picked up the card and read the name. 'Stephen St Clair. Is this the Byte Tech guy?'

Emma batted her eyelashes. 'The sly fox forgot to cancel his card.'

'Look, I don't want any trouble.'

Emma shrugged. 'He has more money than God, thanks to me, and he won't notice.'

In a surprising move, Ben shrugged and processed the payment on Stephen's Amex.

———

For the next thirty minutes, Emma sat beside Dotty—at her insistence—ate lunch, and sipped her third cup of green tea, listening to the raindrops hit the glass of the bay window behind her. Not a single deliveryman from DishNDash arrived at the front of the store to collect orders. The remaining ham-cheese-and-tomato baguettes were left unwanted in the glass cabinet. What a scammer.

The second Emma finished chewing, Dotty peered up at

her. 'Have you been to Turning Pages? It's the most beautiful bookshop in all of Hampshire.'

What a fascinating conversation starter. Could she have heard the drama through the adjoining wall? Or was Dotty sharing that because Emma arrived at the Berry Crumb from that direction?

Emma nodded. 'Yes, I was just in there. There are so many books.'

Dotty turned her head and peered down at Emma's lap. 'But you didn't buy anything?'

'What about you? Did you get anything interesting from the bookshop?'

'Oh yes.' Dotty's face lit up like the first lighting of a town-square Christmas tree. 'I got my hands on a new release. It's crime fiction by Viscount Charles Thomas Worthington the Third. And I'm going to a signing in that awful Leaf & Leather in Little Oak.'

'Is that bookshop no good?' Emma asked, crossing her fingers in hopes that the question alone would be enough for Dotty to spill the beans.

Dotty shook her head. 'That dreadful woman, Victoria Paige, was in Turning Pages, checking out the competition. Just near the till.'

'You mean near the rare books section and the signed copies?'

'Oh yes, but she was a little farther along, pulling out copies of Charles's books, inspecting the signatures, then putting them back.' Dotty shook her head. 'The way she was handling those books was deplorable.'

Emma picked up her teacup and cradled it. 'There was no one in the shop when I was there. It was all deserted and sad.'

Dotty frowned. 'It's a shame, really, because I adore Elsie. She loves books, has a minimalist wardrobe, and wears things over and over again, unlike the youth of today with their disposable clothing. She's quite frugal, you know.'

Emma shuddered. Dotty was dangerous. She knew everything about everyone and didn't seem to think before she shared the intimate details of the private lives of others. Great for amateur sleuthing, bad for keeping scandalous details close to home.

'It was a bit like a Shakespearean tragedy with C-grade actors.' Dotty sighed. 'I wish their sales would pick up. I don't want to go all the way to L & L in Little Oak for a decent read.'

'So it was just you and Victoria in the shop?' Emma took a sip. 'That must have been awkward.'

Dotty's hand shook as she picked up her teapot and poured another cup of black tea. It must have been English Breakfast. 'Well, it was more awkward for Lord Harrington. Victoria caught him on the rolling ladder on the right-hand side of the store.' Dotty leaned in a little closer and whispered, 'He's been looking at rare books at both stores. Honestly, I don't blame him. Victoria's selection is ghastly.'

The china clinked as Emma rested the teacup on its saucer. 'What do you mean?'

'Dear, her idea of rare books is older copies from 1996. She has a US edition of *The Great Gatsby* from 1996, hardback, not-so-great condition.' Dotty slapped her hand on the table, rattling the china. 'And she has the sheer cheek to charge seven thousand pounds for it.'

That was the pricing for an edition from the nineties?

Emma leaned back and listened to the rain for a few moments. 'Did Elsie and Noelle see Victoria in the store?'

Dotty waved her hand dismissively. 'That Noelle is completely inept. She knows nothing about books and has that expensive phone that she is always glued to like burnt cheese on a grill.' Dotty shook her finger at Emma. 'And lives on her own in that flat on her tenner-an-hour wage. That young thing is living above her means.'

Ben chuckled as he sauntered into the kitchen with a new set of tongs and began preparing two orders, which Emma assumed were takeaways. He pulled from under the counter a sheet of off-white paper, then leaned forward, grabbed a baguette with the tongs, and placed it in front of him.

'What?' Emma peered across the room at him.

He threw up his hands in mock surrender, his usual cheeky grin still present. It must be a permanent feature. 'I'm laughing at how you and Dotty are getting worked up over books.'

Emma narrowed her eyes. 'If that bookshop next door closes, all your walk-in customers who order takeaway coffees and sandwiches will dry up.' Emma raised her eyebrows. 'And if I'm not mistaken, that would be your entire customer base.'

Ben winked at Emma. 'Turning Pages is not going out of business with the pompous so-and-so walking past every day, sometimes twice a day, shopping.'

Emma grimaced. 'Are you referring to Lord George Harrington?'

'Yes, that distinguished man of leisure.' Ben shrugged as he pulled a sheet of off-white paper from under the bench and laid it flat on the cutting board. 'He came in one day asking for hot water in a takeaway cup. He sat right there.' Ben pointed at their table. 'The man had the nerve to pull out a tea bag from his waistcoat pocket and make a cup of tea in front of me. But next door, he'll buy a book every other day.'

Ben wrapped up the baguettes, pulled a knife out from under the bench, and cut them in half. Paper bags rustled as Ben packaged the orders. After throwing a fistful of napkins into each bag, Ben grabbed both bags by their handles, walked to the checkout counter, and placed them down with a *thud*.

Emma considered driving to Leaf & Leather and checking out the competition. The whole situation with George Harrington made no sense. Why would he need to travel past multiple times a day? And then there was Miss Noelle—no shop assistant on minimum wage could afford to live in their own flat. Any one of those three could've stolen *The Great Gatsby*, but for different reasons. Would Victoria be so brazen as to stock the stolen book in her shop? Perhaps a visit to Little Oak was in order.

## Chapter Five



Little Oak's town square was exactly what Emma had expected except for one thing—it was more triangular. On its second longest and shortest sides, which formed a right angle, were quaint shops with impeccable storefronts arranged around a central stone war memorial topped with a royal-looking cross. Along the hypotenuse was a narrow two-lane road with parking on either side, uncreatively titled 'High Street.' At least Saint James Upon Berry was original, albeit quirky in naming its laneways.

The same dark clouds loomed overhead, delivering rain to the bare streets. A couple of people sat at a bench in front of the square's only coffee shop, the Daily Grind, near the lower right-hand corner of the square, peering at the rain hitting the cobblestone streets.

Forty-five minutes after leaving the Berry Crumb, Emma drove into Little Oak and spent ten more minutes searching for a parking space. But her luck soon changed when a parking space opened up along High Street opposite the war memorial.

Exiting her car, she pulled up the hood of her rain parka and spotted an electric-vehicle charging station hidden by the hideous yellow Mini behind her. Even though it charged an extortionate sixty pence per kilowatt hour, Emma was relieved at the opportunity to recharge the battery. She suspected she would be in Hampshire for a little longer than an overnight visit. She didn't fancy having to call a mobile service to come and rescue her if her car battery was depleted. How humiliating. She would rather push her car back to London than make that call.

After plugging in the car, Emma used her smartphone to prepay for the service so that the charging could begin. She waltzed across the two-lane High Street, and a small red car with a rounded roof slammed on its brakes and tooted its horn.

She paused on the edge of the town square. On the opposite side of the road was an antique shop with large Georgian windows displaying delicate porcelain and gleaming silverware in the left-hand window. Harrington & Co. Fine Antiquities was an interesting discovery, but it had to wait for another time or at least until after she visited Leaf & Leather. But a little bit of window-shopping had never killed anyone.

After stepping off the edge of the square, Emma strolled across the ancient cobblestone street as she gripped the edge of her hood. The street was permanently closed to vehicles, as evidenced by the circular metal poles protruding from the ground at the junction where High Street met the unnamed pedestrian laneway. She stood in front of the right-hand shop window. Through the glass, she spotted a first-edition Hemingway propped on a velvet stand. The display made her pause.

That window would be the perfect showcase for the stolen *Gatsby* if someone wanted to sell it. Emma dismissed the thought—the last thing she needed was to sound like Dotty with her wild theories. No one would take her seriously. A Lord wouldn't risk his reputation so publicly, especially in a town only thirty minutes away by car. And that might not even be his shop. After all, Harrington was an old English surname with a rich history. Thousands of people might have that surname, and the person running the shop might not even be related.

On the street corner, a white-and-brown Tudor-style building beckoned. Its mediaeval-like facade was in stark contrast to the mixture of Georgian and more modern buildings surrounding it. Hanging from a post above its open wooden door was a simple sign with a leaf bearing an inscription. Underneath the leaf was what appeared to be a hand-drawn book lying on its side with a spine bearing a scribble that was probably supposed to represent a medieval manuscript. The inscription read 'Leaf & Leather.' It was the tackiest logo Emma had ever seen, and that included Byte Tech's first logo, which she'd designed in Microsoft Paint at eighteen.

———

The old wooden floorboards creaked as Emma wandered around the lower level. Apart from the mandatory books in the front shop window, the entire ground floor seemed stuffed with bookish merch. Toys, weird knickknacks, board games, and those strange tiny books one bought for the family bookworm as Christmas stocking stuffers were neatly arranged on the large square, dark-stained oak merchandise tables and the matching wooden bookshelves that lined the room's perimeter.

A couple of elderly patrons walked around the lower

level, picking up items, flipping them over, then putting things down in the wrong place. It was enough to drive Emma bonkers. Taking a deep breath, she inhaled the pungent aroma of orange blossom, cedar, and vanilla.

At the entrance was a massive calendar listing all the store's events. It included everything from poetry readings to the latest book launch for Charles Thomas Worthington III, a regular Saturday evening trivia night, and a murder mystery lock-in, which was coming up on Friday. The last week in January was blocked off as Epic Fantasy Week. It wasn't the worst marketing strategy, and Emma found herself coming up with ideas for Turning Pages. But then, she stopped herself. Why was she so invested in a bookshop she had visited only once, one run by a complete stranger?

As she ambled through the store, her eyes spotted something that, on the surface, seemed innocent but, with all the other puzzle pieces she had assembled, seemed suspicious. Or maybe she was entering her gossipy-old-lady phase three decades too early. At least she would have good company.

According to the obnoxious signage around the store, Leaf Discount Day fell on the first Tuesday of every month. Every Leaf member got ten percent off all purchases for that day only. To sign up for the 'exclusive' membership, customers could join via the Leaf app and pay the one-off joining fee, setting them back a tenner. Yes, Leaf & Leather charge its patrons a tenner for the privilege of joining a bookshop's mailing list. Because that was what it was—a fancy, over-the-top mailing list. It was so sleazy that Emma half expected a complimentary set of steak knives upon sign-up.

But apart from books, one thing was missing—the staff. The antique mahogany checkout counter at the front of the store was unmanned. On either side of the counter were computer-like tills, and in the centre was a round brass bell mounted on black plastic. The tonne of bookish items, the membership fee, the events, and the absence of staff painted two possible pictures: either a cleverly orchestrated marketing scheme or a bookshop struggling to keep its doors open.

As Emma meandered through the tables of merchandise, she spotted a small area with a makeshift wall made of dark-stained oak bookshelves. On one side were soft children's toys, and inside was children's literature. In the centre of the room were tiny chairs and tables with board books scattered across them. Towards the far corner, near a black door that read 'Staff Only,' was a tiny woman with shoulder-length brown hair and a waist that Emma would happily sell her mother to possess. Her mother would understand, of course.

Emma strolled into the children's department and almost tripped over a small plastic chair lying on its back on the wooden floor. The floor creaked, and the petite woman turned around. Dressed in all black from head to toe, she wore a frilled-edge beige apron with green leaves printed on it and the words Leaf & Leather in a modern font.

'Welcome to Leaf & Leather. I'm the manager, Victoria Paige.' Victoria smiled, but it didn't reach her eyes.

But that was to be expected because that was probably the hundredth time she had said that exact phrase for the day.

'This store is locally owned and operated,' Victoria shared, possibly in an attempt to fill the awkward silence or guilt her into making a purchase on the way out.

Emma peered around the room. 'Do you have a rare-book section, by any chance? I'm looking for a gift for my mother. It's her birthday.' Emma overshared, hoping that she would come across as a genuine customer.

Victoria beamed. 'We have quite a few signed editions

upstairs, some of which are several decades old.' She gestured for Emma to follow her as she dashed across the room and up the stairs.

Wheezing, Emma darted up the wide staircase made from wood a little darker than the shelves. The miniature landing bore a table with leaflets advertising local events. Emma slowed to a jog and climbed up a second flight of stairs. As she reached the second level, she surveyed the expansive area. That was where the actual bookshop began and ended.

Apart from the large windows at the front of the shop, the remaining walls were lined with books. In the centre were four massive tables featuring face-up paperbacks, with bright-green buy-one-get-one-half-price stickers. Maybe Emma's theory about a struggling bookshop wasn't so far-fetched. Weaving between the four tables, Emma followed Victoria to a bookcase near the front right-hand corner of the room.

Victoria pointed at the shelves. 'Here we have many first editions of Charles Thomas Worthington the Third's first books. Most are from the 1990s, complete with authentic signatures.'

'How can you tell if it's authentic or not?' Emma asked as Victoria opened her mouth.

'Our most famous local, Lord George Harrington, is a retired historian who runs an antique store in the square. Usually, I take them to him, and he appraises them for me and often suggests a price.'

Emma nodded. 'Oh, it must be handy having him nearby.'

'Oh yes.' Victoria flashed that same fake smile that didn't touch her eyes.

'You don't have anything older?' Emma scanned the shelves. 'I was looking for an older edition of *The Great Gatsby*, my mother's favourite book. It doesn't have to be signed or anything. Or even a special modern edition with illustrations.'

Victoria held up her finger and beamed once more. That time, she seemed legitimately happy. Like a little mouse being chased by a cat, she scurried along the bookshelves on the right-hand side of the room to a checkout counter in front of a large dark-stained cabinet with doors. Within a few minutes, she'd unlocked the cabinet doors with a key from the front pocket of her apron then returned holding a hardback edition with that infamous blue cover.

'It's a US printing from 1996, but it's in relatively good condition with no writing in the margins.' Victoria opened the book and flipped through its pages. 'I believe it was sourced from an estate sale in New York while Lord Harrington was on holiday.'

Emma furrowed her brow. 'Why didn't he sell it in his antique shop?'

'Oh no.' Victoria waved dismissively. 'He only sells antiques.'

'What if I wanted something from the first print run or around the year of publication, say, 1925?' Emma tilted her head.

Victoria's slender frame tensed, then she chuckled. 'You won't find anything like that around here.' Victoria paused. 'I can't think of anywhere local that you could go. Maybe at an auction at Christie's in London? And if anything like that existed locally, Lord Harrington would've purchased it long ago.' Victoria leaned in. 'He's quite the fan, perhaps like your mother.'

Emma sighed. 'Not even at a small bookshop in a neighbouring town?'

Victoria's eyes bulged. 'I don't have time to visit other bookshops. I'm too busy with my baby.' She gestured around the room then stormed off to the cabinet.

The woman had just looked Emma straight in the eye and lied. She'd gotten all offended over a question any customer would ask if a bookshop didn't have the book they wanted. How strange. There was something weird going on in these bookshops. Maybe it was time to have a chinwag with the local aristocrat.

## Chapter Six

### BEYOND THE SHOP WINDOW

*B*efore walking back through the first and ground floors of Leaf & Leather, Emma pulled a signed paperback off the shelf. It was a 1997 edition of *Last Night* by Charles Thomas Worthington III. Inside the cover, after the blank page, the author's signature was scrawled across the page between the title and the publisher's name. Much to Victoria's delight, Emma purchased it.

The edition set her back seven hundred and fifty pounds. Emma almost cried as she ran the purchase through on her new black Amex—the one with her name on it, not the one that belonged to that sly fox of a man. The purchase seemed to make amends with Victoria, and the woman acted as if the awkward questioning had never happened. With a wave from Victoria, Emma wandered through the shop and onto the street, clutching a complimentary book bag. Inside it was a box containing the signed copy.

After stuffing it inside her rain parka, Emma dashed out of the shop and followed the pedestrian cobblestone street to the antique shop. She paused outside the large Georgian windows and gazed at the antique chess set on display. It was a relic from a bygone era, something that belonged in a stately home where the staff lived in the basement and the aristocracy was served breakfast in bed every morning.

Emma shuddered as she considered the price. Even though she had a massive settlement coming her way, she knew half of it would be taken by HMRC, so she wasn't in the market for more expensive items.

With her left hand stuffed inside her stone rain parka, clutching the book bag, Emma walked over to the black-painted wooden front door. The rain had soaked a plastic open sign that hung off the door's large frosted-glass-panelled window. She gripped the handle and opened the door, triggering the brass wooden bell, then stepped inside.

'I'll be right there,' a voice called from behind the doorless wall. Clanging and grinding of metal could be heard from within the back room. The noise was so loud that it was difficult to hear the rest of the man's conversation.

Soft-yellow lantern-style sconces hung from curved brass hooks mounted on the oak walls and lit the shop's interior. In the centre, a couple of metres from the door, was an antique desk made from a similar oak-like material with a green banker lamp to the left. On the right-hand side of the desk was a thin, closed laptop and a tiny plastic credit card reader. One of those modern fancy ones, it had a large panel for customers to tap, a small screen, and a number pad.

Along the left-hand side of the small shop floor, multiple large paintings were stacked on each other and propped against the wall. In front of those paintings was an old globe with a vast open ocean space in the southern hemisphere.

Next to the globe was a polished antique red oak safe, its door ajar. Another chessboard sat on top of the safe, the pieces lined up as if hoping to be played. To her left was an old green chaise longue. Its fabric resembled velvet, but she dared not sit on it for fear that Lord George Harrington had a 'you sit, you pay' policy.

Emma pulled the book bag out of her rain parka and held it as she surveyed the shop. From the outside, the shop seemed larger. Perhaps the back room was a workshop or storeroom filled with more antique furniture and other large pieces.

The wall popped open. A short man with a thick head of grey hair entered the space, and he wore a three-piece suit and a pocket watch. As the door closed, a sea of mismatched furniture and a large machine caught Emma's eye. At the back of the store was a machine made from redwood with a cast-iron base, a large black cylinder that might be some kind of drum, and a massive metal tray. It looked like an industrial assembly-line machine from the twenties, something that belonged in a museum.

'Is there something I can help you with, miss?' He peered at her over the tops of his small, rectangular, rimless spectacles. 'I'm George Harrington, the owner of this fine establishment.'

'I was just in the bookshop.' Emma pointed down the street.

George reached for her book bag. 'Show me what you got.' He eagerly grabbed the bag from her hand, unravelled it, pulled out the box, and opened it. 'Oh, this was one of mine,' he exclaimed. 'I had the old bugger sign it at the end of the nineties. Just between you and me, old Charles is quite the pill. But you know what they say. There's a fine line between genius and madness.'

An anecdote about the signature did add to its authenticity, but it was a bit over the top and was quite an aggressive thing to say about a local author. George's familiarity with Charles suggested a personal connection. Perhaps their shared aristocratic status had led them to rub shoulders. Or a falling-out had soured their relationship.

On top of that, Lord Harrington's warmth and friendliness contrasted sharply with Ben and Dotty's warnings. Their assessment of his character didn't quite add up.

Emma smiled politely as George placed the book back in its box. 'Actually, I was looking for a rare first edition, and Victoria pointed me in your direction.'

George placed the box inside the bag. 'Wanting to start your collection?'

'Well, it's for my mother.' Emma nodded.

'If you're looking for rare first editions, I insist'—George cleared his throat—'that you check out a little gem of a place in Saint James Upon Berry called Turning Pages.' He shook his finger at her. 'Be warned, you'll never want to leave.' He paused then handed the book bag to Emma. 'Actually, I don't understand why Victoria didn't recommend it to you. I saw her there this morning.' George winked at her. 'She was checking out the competition. It's a proper independent bookshop. It closes at six, so you have time.'

'I was wondering'—Emma peered over at George, who had leaned in a little closer— 'do you have any tips on authenticating older books, say, from the twenties or thirties?'

George removed his glasses, held them out, squinted, then polished them with his waistcoat. 'Short of having a degree or three in history, you'll need to get it appraised by an expert. You see, it's all about the paper and the lettering. The printing style from that era is quite distinct.' He paused as he put on his glasses. 'That's better,' he said with a smile. 'Even I get something appraised before purchasing, and I'm a retired historian. In my fifties, I did a second PhD after falling in love with the 1920s. It was an interesting time period. I won't bore you with the details.' He nodded. 'If you do go to Turning Pages and see something you like, let me know. I'll stop by and check it out for you then let you know if I think it's a worthwhile purchase. Every now and then, I go to the store and check things out for prospective buyers.' Leaning forward, George opened a drawer under the antique desk's tabletop and rummaged around.

So, that was why he went to Turning Pages so often. He had a side hustle of appraising books and probably charged a fee. There she was, moments earlier, thinking he had stolen something to sell in his antique shop.

He handed her a business card. 'My services aren't free, naturally, but my rates are reasonable. Turning Pages has a rare first edition of *Alice's Adventures in Wonderland*. It's one of the recalled first printings. The price is quite steep. That one is worth it, provided you can shell out the cash.'

Emma nodded. 'What about author signatures? How can you tell if they're real?'

George shrugged. 'Honestly, a master forger can fool some experts. It takes time to study the signature and ink, and you have to allow for anomalies because no one signs their name exactly the same every time.' George tapped the wrapped-up book in her hands. 'That one, my dear, is very real.'

Maybe he did know his stuff. Emma peered at the Edwardian-looking font on the business card and sighed. The interview hadn't turned out the way she had hoped. She'd expected to speak with a villain, but he was nothing more than a historian who loved books.

'I should let you go.' Emma sighed. 'Oh, by the way, I noticed you have a lot of furniture and a massive machine in the back.'

George's eyes widened. 'That, my dear, is a printing press from back in the day when one had to arrange the individual letters on a tray and then press the machine onto a page that was fed through the machine.' He nodded. 'It's broken, and I'm desperately hoping to restore it. My wife won't let me keep it at home, so it lives in my storage room here. It's quite the money vacuum.'

'That's fascinating.' Emma gestured towards the back room. 'I'd love to see it working someday.'

'Honestly, me too.' George's enthusiasm appeared to dim. 'The restoration is taking longer than expected. Parts from the 1920s aren't exactly easy to come by.' He tugged on the chain of his pocket watch, flipped it open, and glanced at the time. 'Speaking of time, you should head to Turning Pages before closing, especially if you want to see the first edition of *Alice's Adventures in Wonderland* and have enough time to inspect it. Do give my regards to Elsie.'

As Emma stepped back onto the rain-slicked cobble-stones, she couldn't shake the feeling that everyone was playing their part—and playing it a little too perfectly. And she couldn't help feeling like she was being pushed out of the door. Or maybe that was her newfound overactive imagination. There was the helpful aristocrat, the competitive book-shop owner, and the struggling twentysomething shopkeeper. Everyone had means, motive, and opportunity. One of them must be playing a part, hoping not to get caught.

At least her trip to Little Oak yielded two positives: a fully charged car and the rain had stopped. She had time to return to Turning Pages before closing. But one final decision still loomed. Should she tell Elsie about her findings or wait for the security system to be installed?

# Chapter Seven

## A BITTER BREW

*E*mma walked across the town square with her signed paperback tucked under her arm. Light raindrops fell from the sky—not again. A nearby brass bell jangled. She peered over her shoulder towards the lower right-hand corner of the square as the front door to the Daily Grind opened. The scents of ground coffee beans, cinnamon, and melted chocolate mingled with the smell of rain. The delicious aroma lured her across the square and into the shop.

Before she had a chance to reassess her priorities, Emma reached out to open the front door. Sure, she should return to Turning Pages, but the winter chill made her crave something hot. And the bookshop closed at six, so she had plenty of time to drive back.

Tugging on the door handle, Emma opened the door, triggering the brass bell. She slipped inside the shop. The place was empty apart from a shaggy-haired barista dressed in all black with a navy apron around his neck and tied around his waist. He darted around the seating in the front of the shop, clearing the tables. He paused, peered over at her, smiled, and continued carrying out his duties then wandered towards the passageway and took a sharp right.

A simple chalkboard menu listing an array of coffees, teas, and other hot and cold drinks hung on the exposed redbrick wall. The menu spanned three-quarters of the width of the Daily Grind's interior, allowing room for a passageway to a possible back room. To her left was a row of refrigerated ready-to-eat sandwiches and salads. Next to that was a hot-food section with a lonely starter-sized portion of minestrone soup and one ham-and-cheese toasty.

Instead of getting a hot chocolate, Emma picked up the soup and walked towards the counter. She peered down the aisle as she picked a bottle of water out of the doorless refrigerators. An ample seating area was in the back, along with French doors that led to a terrace. Emma placed the soup and the water bottle on the counter and waited for the barista to return.

A few seconds later, he dashed to the counter space, hunched over the cash register, and bashed his finger against the touch screen, causing the screen to wobble. As she waited for him to acknowledge her existence, Emma read the name on his badge: Noa. Underneath that were the words 'Store Manager.'

Noa pushed the card machine towards her, crouched, and rummaged underneath the counter. Awkward didn't even begin to describe the situation. There was no hello or even eye contact, just silence and the occasional hum from the coffee machines and the fridges. After she paid for her soup, Noa slid over a clear plastic spoon-fork on a single napkin bearing the coffee shop logo then ripped off the receipt, scrunched it in his hand, and threw it into the bin.

She wandered along the length of the counter then down the hall towards the back seating area.

'Ah.' Noa stammered from behind her. 'I've just cleaned back there.'

So, he does speak—fascinating. Emma sat at a table for two, facing the glass French doors, watching the raindrops fall onto the outdoor furniture. She ate the soup with her ridiculous spoon-fork, waiting for Noa to insist that she move to the front of the store. But he didn't say another word. And who in their right mind rationed napkins? No wonder the place was empty on a Tuesday afternoon.

As she contemplated getting up and asking for another napkin and an actual spoon, the jangling of the brass bell at the front of the store broke her train of thought. Would this person get the same awkward reception?

'Noa,' a loud, shrill voice said. 'Were you at the Chamber of Commerce meeting last Thursday night? The one in December.'

A loud giggling and the clanking of china filled the silence.

'Oh no. I want my cappuccino to go.' The woman sighed. 'Doesn't matter. I'll drink it here, and we can have a chinwag.' She tapped the counter. 'Honestly, I don't know how much longer I can take that grinding and clanging from that antique store. It's doing my head in. And what is that man doing in there? Is he making antiques? Can you imagine?' the woman said with a gasp.

Emma sipped her soup and turned her ear towards the front of the store. That woman had made Dotty's gossiping habit seem more like a public service. And to some extent, the woman was right. The sounds from George's shop raised questions. Perhaps he truly was desperately trying to restore the antique printing press. Or maybe other antique furniture lay in pieces across his workshop floor.

'Anyway, you probably can't hear him all the way over

here. Lucky you.' The conversation soon reached a lull but was quickly interrupted by a soft clink.

She must be drinking her cappuccino at the counter.

'That petty woman applied for business relief in the third quarter of the previous year, at the same time I did, but I was knocked back, and she was approved. My store, Loop, is struggling. And she sells cheap yarn in that place she dares to call a bookshop.' She let out an exasperated sigh. 'I know this is wrong, but I hoped that eyesore of a business would close. Boy, was I wrong. After the meeting, Victoria was boasting to everyone who had ears. Thanks to her brilliant marketing ideas—her words, not mine—Leaf & Leather's revenue increased by one hundred thousand pounds in quarter four. And that saved the shop.' The woman sounded as if she was going to cry. 'Those ideas aren't even hers. She copied my ideas for my store.'

Emma rolled her eyes as she took another sip of her soup. She cast her mind back to her first impressions of Leaf & Leather. All the so-called brilliant marketing ideas Victoria had set in place could be found in another popular chain of bookshops all over London, so the ideas weren't exclusive to the Loop lady. But could those tactics bring in that much revenue, or was it just Christmas? From an economic perspective, times were tough, and sales for businesses using Byte Tech's technology were down. According to the radio report on the drive to Saint James Upon Berry, Christmas sales from the previous year were down compared to the year before.

Victoria could've easily lied about the timing of the revenue increase. The amount sounded similar to the price of the missing *Gatsby*—it was almost too perfect. The likelihood of someone checking or catching her in the lie was low. Also, Leaf & Leather was an independent bookshop, not a publicly traded company. No quarterly reports would be sent to shareholders. Thus, no one would know when the revenue came in besides HMRC and maybe the Chamber of Commerce. It would be the ideal lie to cover up the *Gatsby* sale.

## Chapter Eight

TURNING THE PAGE

For the next thirty minutes, Emma was held hostage by the owner of Loop, who, during her endless babble, had identified herself as Margaret. There was no way Emma could leave the Daily Grind without the woman realising that she had been listening the entire time. Emma had half considered visiting Loop to see if she could get more dirt on Victoria or George Harrington.

But Margaret seemed determined to share every grievance she'd accumulated since she'd first taken a breath, then she returned to the topic of Loop. Emma's bowl of minestrone soup sat empty as she waited for the woman to run out of either gossip or breath. As Margaret finally left, Noa broke his silence and said, 'Goodbye, Margaret,' but it was spoken in a tone that conveyed, 'Don't come again, Margaret.' The monologue from hell had finally ended and not a moment too soon.

Emma rose from her small table in the back of the coffee shop, meandered towards the front, and dumped the soup bowl in the bin. Her mind still churned over Victoria's suspicious revenue claims. To sell a first edition of a *Gatsby* would require careful planning—selling it online, perhaps, or by auction in London? And would someone have to provide proof of ownership to sell by auction?

Standing at the door, Emma peered out and watched the raindrops hit the cobblestones in the pedestrian street. It hadn't stopped raining like she had hoped. As Emma put on her rain parka, her smartphone buzzed as a doorbell-like chime broke the silence of the coffee shop. A text had come through. She slipped out her smartphone, tapped the screen, and opened a message. It was from Elsie.

> I'm sorry, but it was far too expensive. I've been reviewing my books and can't justify the expense, even though it's for a worthy cause.

Emma sighed as she stared at the message on her screen. Of course Elsie couldn't drop one hundred pounds on cameras at a moment's notice. The poor woman could barely keep her beloved bookshop afloat. Emma's chest tightened. But Turning Pages needed those security cameras.

Through the rain-streaked windows, she spotted a bright-blue neon Open sign. She leaned forward and squinted. Her hot breath fogged up a small patch of the door's window. She beamed. A solution had materialised. Emma didn't know why she hadn't thought of it before.

Little Oak's town square had an electronics shop that was in the centre of a row of businesses opposite the tall war memorial. Bytes & Bits Electronics was wedged between Pizza Palace and Loop. The gold font of the shop sign blended with the building, but the flat-screen TV and display of DSLR cameras in the floor-to-ceiling bay windows clashed with the Georgian facade.

Both shops had darkened windows, but the electronics shop was open. If Emma bought the cameras, she and Elsie could install them that afternoon instead of waiting for the money to be free in the store's budget. It was perfect. But would Elsie see it as overstepping or take it as a friendly gesture?

Maybe she could put that sly fox's hush money to good use after all. To be honest, that was exactly what it was—payment for her silence. After sliding the hood of her rain parka over her head, Emma stepped out into the rain and across the town square.

———

*Ding, ding.* The tiny brass bell over the door of Turning Pages rang as Emma stepped inside with three tiny high-definition security cameras, a little over an hour and a few hundred pounds later. From the second she'd seen them in Bytes & Bits, Emma had known they were perfect for the shop. They boasted of twelve hours of continuous filming on a single battery charge. Not only that, but they were also small enough to mount to the side roof of the bookshelves and fit between the hanging strip and the top of the books.

After setting the cameras on the counter, Emma quickly stepped back outside, slipped off her coat, and shook the rain off as she leaned against the door, holding it open. Then with a bang, the door closed behind her. She hung her parka on the rustic solid oak coatrack.

'Just a moment,' Noelle called out from the back of the store.

Emma sauntered up the three steps between the entry and the main floor and gazed around at the breathtaking rustic oak bookshelves. The small literary haven deserved to be saved. Not only that, but Leaf & Leather was too far away for local residents like Dotty to shop there. Emma was determined to save Turning Pages from closure and prevent any further thefts.

The floorboards creaked as she wandered past the shop's only checkout counter. She entered the maze of shelves, stopping every so often as a book's spine lured her closer.

'Noelle, Elsie!' she yelled as she continued to waltz through the maze of aisles as they twisted and turned towards the stockroom at the back of the shop.

The more Emma soaked in the shop's atmosphere, the more she couldn't help thinking of how some of Victoria's ideas to bring customers into the shop could help save Turning Pages—not having an endless supply of knickknacks but hosting literary trivia nights, murder mystery lock-ins, and other events of that nature. All she had to do was remove a few bookshelves, have a buy-one-get-one-half-price sale, and put the rest of the books in the storeroom. She would have all that room for events.

'Emma, you're back.' Noelle blushed. 'Did you check out Ben? I know he's far too old for me, but I love to look at him. He's so pretty.'

Emma bit the side of her lip. 'Yeah, he has some appeal. But what worries me more is that he's praying-mantis-shaped and a pastry chef. That shouldn't be allowed.'

With a giggle, Noelle said, 'I assure you, he bakes everything himself the day before and the morning of.' Noelle shrugged. 'I work there a couple of hours from five till opening, then I work here,' she said in a hushed tone.

So, that's how she affords her flat. Perhaps she'd judged Noelle too harshly?

'What's in there?' Noelle pointed at the bag in Emma's hand.

'Oh.' Emma opened the bag and showed Noelle. 'I thought since Elsie couldn't afford to buy the cameras, I could buy them for Turning Pages as a gift.'

'You have no idea how much this means to me. I've been looking for other jobs, fearing Turning Pages would close,' Noelle blubbered. 'I just love this store. Elsie will be so over-joyed. This shop is everything to her.'

Emma wrapped her right arm around Noelle, who collapsed onto her shoulder and sobbed even louder. So that was what she had been doing on her phone earlier that day, looking for another job. Even with the revelation, something wasn't quite adding up. It was the same feeling Emma had had before discovering that Sly Fox was cheating. At first, she'd thought Human Resources was helping him cover up a scandal—one of those 'cancelled for all time' scandals. But she'd soon found out that she was wrong and a little right all at the same time. Emma didn't think Noelle was as innocent as she seemed, and the feeling was one she couldn't shake. And she wouldn't bury her head in the sand and pretend the hunch didn't exist.

Noelle grabbed the bag out of Emma's hands. 'We should set them up while Elsie does last week's banking in Little Oak. And we can surprise her when she gets back. I can't wait to see the look on her face.'

'Yeah, that sounds great. We could mount them on the inside roof of the bookshelves and let them hang below the hanging strip, just above the books. They won't be seen easily. But you'll need to charge them every twelve hours,' Emma said as Noelle peered into the bag and jiggled the contents around.

'I used to work in a hardware store'—Noelle beamed—'so I can get the tool kit from the stockroom and help you.'

Before Emma could respond, Noelle sprinted through the maze and towards the back stockroom. Maybe it was time and age that had made Emma so suspicious of Noelle. On the one hand, she seemed legitimately excited and relieved. That nagging sensation crept in—the same one that Emma had ignored the day that sly fox hired that twentysomething leggy thing. The choice loomed: trust that feeling or give Noelle the benefit of the doubt.

# Chapter Nine

## BETWEEN THE SHELVES

The windowless stockroom at Turning Pages was little more than a glorified closet, barely wide enough for two people to stand in side by side. It ran along the entire length of the shop and had no back door, so stock had to be brought into the store through the front doors. Empty cardboard boxes were flattened and stacked against the back wall, waiting to be recycled. The musty aroma of cardboard boxes mingled with the sharp scent of cleaning supplies and a faint hint of dust that seemed to cling to the surface of every piece of furniture.

In the corner of the stockroom, in the ceiling was an attic-style door, where an internal staircase once was, and a fold-up ladder. The owners of the shop space must be renting out the top floor to a separate tenant. It wasn't uncommon to find flat rentals located in high streets above a Little Waitrose or a hair salon. The location wasn't ideal, but the rents were cheaper.

A lone metal shelving unit held an open box containing a few paper bags bearing the shop's logo. Next on the shelf was another box filled with cotton tote bags. A thin layer of dust was sprinkled across the top of the box. Filled to the brim, the box gave the impression it had been opened weeks ago, but not a single bag had ever been sold to a customer. Cleaning supplies and a battered first aid kit, also collecting dust, sat between the box of cotton tote bags and a torn box of cash register rolls. There were no boxes of books.

The entirety of the shop's stock was out on the shelves. Perhaps the stockroom's size was the reason for the maze of bookshelves. One would never know that they were in the stockroom of a bookshop. The stockroom's scant furniture included the world's squeakiest desk chair, which probably came flat-packed. A bright-pink exercise ball sat beside the chair and leaned against the small desk's drawers. A desktop computer sat on the table between two black trays filled with papers from the Dark Ages, pages Elsie had used for inventory and ordering. It had been almost an hour since Emma had mounted the three cameras, synced them to the computer via Bluetooth, jailbroke the in-house software, and added it to Byte Tech's forever beta program, all under the watchful eye of Noelle. Outside, the rain had ceased, but the threatening thick grey clouds remained.

Standing behind the squeaky chair, Emma stared at the software as it loaded on the screen. Byte Tech's white logo spun on a primary-blue background as the software continued to load. Emma paced along the length of the stockroom. She couldn't bear to watch the logo a second longer. It was a permanent reminder of a former life that was gone forever. A hollow, heavy sensation grew in her chest. She blinked back the tears and cast her mind over the events that had taken place since she'd first walked into Turning Pages.

'It worked,' Noelle squealed. 'You're a genius.'

Emma took a deep breath. Turning, Emma glanced at the full-colour image on the screen. She had a full view of the thick layers of dust that lined the tops of the bookshelves and a partial view of the aisles. A fourth or potential fifth camera was needed, especially if Elsie was going to prevent thefts from the rare-book section in the future. But that would do for the time being.

Emma wandered across the room, pulled out the chair, and sat. Noelle hunched over, resting her elbows on the desk, her eyes fixed on the screen.

Emma struck the arrow keys and flicked between the various camera views before settling on the four-grid layout with the fourth quarter blackened out. She pointed at the camera displays. 'The screen's resolution leaves a lot to be desired, but the smartphone app will be much clearer.' Emma tapped the arrows on the keyboard and changed the angle of the camera mounted above the rare-books section. 'I placed this camera above the rare-books section so you could see the face of the person browsing the shelves. But we could put a camera in the other direction, facing the shelf, if you like.'

'So, we can only have four cameras?' Noelle pointed at the blacked-out grid in the screen's lower right-hand corner.

Noelle's initial excitement seemed to wane. Her sudden interest in the security systems limitations felt calculated. A concerned employee would focus on using the camera, not their limitations. It was hard to gauge what was going on with Noelle. She seemed to play both parts well—the eager assistant and the overly curious observer.

'You can connect up to nine cameras with this software. It's the beta edition. Users receive the latest not-released features before they are rolled out to the general public.' Emma peered over at Noelle, who was still watching the camera feeds. 'But if you upgrade, you can get more cameras. So, it's not a problem.'

'That's good news.' Noelle nodded. 'I wish we'd had these cameras before the first edition was stolen.'

Emma narrowed her eyes. Maybe she had misjudged Noelle. Possibly. 'How often did Lord Harrington visit the shop and look at the *Gatsby*?'

Noelle's eyes widened. 'Is that who you think stole the book?'

Emma sighed. Should she be sharing this? Probably not. But Noelle's reaction might indicate whether she was working with someone like Lord Harrington or Victoria. 'I was in his antique shop this afternoon, and he has an old broken printing press. He claims to be working on it.'

Noelle gasped. 'He could be attempting to forge the book.'

'Technically, other shop owners in the area heard loud noises from the back of his shop. But that's not confirmation that the printing press is in working order. But it might support his claims of working on the press.' Emma glanced at the screen then refocused on Noelle, who had hunched over and rested her chin on her arms, which were folded into a makeshift pillow. She seemed bored.

A dull jingling from the front door's brass bell, the slamming of a door, and a series of heavy footfalls interrupted Emma's train of thought. The shop's second camera was mounted under the hanging strip of the corner bookshelf in the back right-hand corner of the store and pointed towards the front door. On the screen, via the second-camera feed, a head of hair moved between the shelves. The camera angle was too high. Emma had forgotten about the shop floor and the books. Maybe the aisle was more important.

They needed another camera focused on the door and another facing the rare-books section, so that was two more cameras, bringing the count to five. A sixth was needed for the back corner, and a seventh was needed above the checkout counter. Were armed robberies still a thing? Better to be safe than sorry. Turning Pages required a seven-camera system. Was that going overboard?

Noelle nudged Emma with her right elbow. 'Is that—' she whispered as she pressed a finger to her lips.

A thick head of grey hair obscured the camera's view of the front door. Someone had climbed the rolling library ladder in the left-corner bookshelf on the right-hand side of the store. Emma was certain she knew who it was, and she suspected that the individual also owned the expensive-looking navy scarf she'd seen hanging on the ladder when she first walked into the shop a little before midday.

Emma's heart raced as the head of hair disappeared from the camera's view. The figure strolled through the store and paused as they reached the checkout counter. Turning, the figure glanced around the shop as if looking for someone. The light from the late afternoon streamed through the shop's window, obstructing their view of the person's face.

Emma bit back a gasp. She would have recognised that figure anywhere, especially after her earlier encounters. Lord Harrington had returned, probably to retrieve his navy scarf from the ladder. Still, something about his presence in the shop caused her pulse to quicken.

Noelle grabbed Emma's arm. 'What are we going to do? Should we confront him?'

Emma froze as she watched the figure pace. She tapped the arrow keys on the keyboard and toggled the camera angle. The figure, probably growing bored of waiting, turned and faced the camera then wandered around the right-hand side of the store. It was George. He reached into his pocket, pulled out something small, then peered down at it—it must be his pocket watch. His frequent glances at his pocket watch suggested more than a casual visit. An appointment, perhaps —though whether with Elsie or a certain young bookshop clerk remained to be seen.

Emma took a deep breath and turned to Noelle. 'Obviously, I can't just leave the stockroom and chat with him.' She paused and watched Noelle's face, but she didn't seem too worried. Noelle was watching the security cameras the same way a couch potato would flick through the channels on the television on a lazy Sunday afternoon, minus the couch and remote. 'How do you feel about chatting with George while I check the bookshelves? I know it's a huge risk, but maybe you could distract him with another purchase.'

Emma grimaced. Sending a young woman to chat with either her partner in crime or with a thief seemed reckless. Noelle could be innocent, and here she was putting her in potential danger. Perhaps Noelle's strange behaviour stemmed from being set up as a convenient scapegoat. Confronting George was a task that rightfully belonged to Emma, but she had no authority there because it wasn't her shop. No plausible excuse existed for her to be chatting with a customer—it had to be Noelle.

'Okay.' Noelle got up and waltzed the length of the stock-room towards the door, her mannerisms a little childlike. The young woman didn't consider the potential danger associated with her actions. Or maybe Noelle and George were working together.

The door to the stockroom shut with a loud *bang*.

With one eye on the screen, Emma pulled out her smart-phone and downloaded the app. She felt uneasy about leaving the stockroom without her eyes on the shop floor. Noelle would be alone, the security cameras unmonitored for only a few minutes, but a lot could happen in a few minutes. Despite Emma's reservations about Noelle's behaviour, she still felt guilty for drawing the young woman into the effort to spy on George, even if she was somehow involved in the theft.

George pulled out his pocket watch, opened it, glanced at it for a second time, then glanced at the door. He didn't seem to be at the shop to buy something, nor was he wandering through the aisles, looking at books or searching for staff. And he hadn't rung the bell. His purpose for being in the store felt more like an appointment than a book lover's casual visit. Something was off. He must be working with someone.

As Emma waited for the app to download on her smartphone, the jingling of the front-door bell caused her to look up at the security camera. A tall, thin older woman with a pink-rinse pixie cut and a navy hooded raincoat dashed through the shop floor, holding a thick wad of pages tucked under her arm. Elsie had returned from the bank.

With a wave, Elsie dashed across the store and around the checkout counter. Placing the pages on the counter, Elsie leaned over and began an intense conversation with George. The *Gatsby* appointment wasn't until tomorrow, yet something urgent passed between them.

In the third camera, Noelle froze, turned around, then sprinted towards the shelves and the ladder. A few moments later, the top of Noelle's head appeared in the view of the second camera. Noelle was checking the shelves in full view of George. Her pulse quickened—if either Elsie or George glanced up, they would spot Noelle immediately.

As Emma watched the conversation unfold, tension coiled in her chest. She tapped the keys at the top of the keyboard and increased the camera's zoom. The intrusion felt wrong—a violation of privacy—but the documents pulled at her curiosity. Something about Elsie's return from the bank with the documents seemed off. Even in business, banking documents were sent electronically, especially contracts for loans and other things of that nature.

With the camera zoomed in, Emma stared at the grainy image and groaned. Her smartphone beeped and buzzed on the table—the software had finished downloading. A few minutes later, she connected the cameras to her phone via the Wi-Fi then waited for them to load.

The wall of the stockroom tremored as the door shut. Emma peered over her shoulder at a wide-eyed Noelle, who came running towards her.

'There's no extra book on the shelf. So, he wasn't returning a forged copy of the *Gatsby*,' Noelle whispered. 'I have no idea—' She froze as she stared at the screen. 'That's the logo of Turning Pages's insurance company.'

A rock formed in the pit of Emma's stomach. No insurance company would process paperwork that quickly for a theft that had happened only hours ago. The claim forms seemed suspicious, and their sudden appearance raised more questions than answers.

Like a cascade of half-formed theories, thoughts popped into Emma's mind like one of those whack-a-mole games at a children's fun zone. Elsie had tried to sell her *The Great Gatsby* despite having an interested party with an evaluation appointment on Wednesday. Why not suggest a modern illustrated edition? Then, she had volunteered information about Lord Harrington's appointment with an eagerness that now seemed calculated.

Most telling, Elsie had been reluctant to purchase cameras after the theft of a first edition priced at over ninety-nine thousand pounds. Tight for cash, perhaps, but wouldn't desperation to prevent future thefts override financial caution? If someone could do it once, wouldn't they return? Each detail aligned like the last three pieces of a thousand-piece jigsaw, forming a pattern too deliberate to be a coincidence.

Then, there were George's daily visits—such strange behaviour. Even if he was evaluating books for other customers, that was still odd. If George had been examining the *Gatsby* for weeks, he would know whether it was genuine. A historian with his expertise wouldn't need multiple visits unless he was documenting it and creating a perfect record of every detail—the kind of record one would need for insurance authentication or something else.

Her eyes widened. Something else—like creating a forgery with that printing press. One detail still nagged at her. While in the Berry Crumb, Ben had said he saw George in the area, sometimes twice a day. There was no way he needed that many visits to document a book unless he was checking on something else, like making sure Elsie had followed through with their plan. They were working together.

The theory felt implausible. A conspiracy over a first-edition *Gatsby* seemed ridiculous. And why would he help Elsie? He had no skin in the game. If her shop closed, it had no bearing on him. Perhaps it was simpler than that.

It could all be about insurance fraud. The day's 'theft' could've been nothing more than a piece of theatre, carefully staged with Emma as an unwitting witness. One would call that corroborating a testimony. And her chat with George might have spooked him. That could also be the reason for his visit. He was probably trying to forge the *Gatsby* with his press and was worried that Elsie would sell it to another customer. Maybe that was why he visited so frequently. He was checking to see if the book was still available.

But one thing was missing—proof. All Emma had was a working theory, substantial, yes, but unverified.

## Chapter Ten

CHAPTER AND VERSE

A thick band formed around Emma's chest as it dawned on her that she was trapped inside the bookshop at seventeen minutes after closing. At least security cameras were monitoring the shop floor. Her heart raced as she glanced at the footage. Elsie wandered around the checkout counter, across the floor, and to the door. Instead of letting George out, she locked it then returned to the counter. Emma was trapped in the bookshop. To some booklovers, being trapped in a bookshop would be a dream come true—but not with two potential felons.

She glanced at the overflowing in-tray on her right. It was driving her spare. How hard was it to organise papers? She grabbed the pages and rearranged them in a neat stack. As she thumbed through the pile, an invoice caught her eye. Within the pile, a company logo, comprised of a thin font, was at the top of many invoices. Emma pulled it out. It read Harrington Holdings, Inc.

So, he did have a vested interest in Turning Pages. He owned the entire building. Given the town's size and the high street location, finding another tenant would be difficult. If Turning Pages went out of business and closed, even with a contract, he could be out of money due to legal fees and missed rent.

Emma had to confront them. It was inevitable. But she had security measures.

'Oh my Gawd,' Noelle whispered from behind Emma's shoulder, making her jump. 'He owns the building, and Elsie is doing something dodgy with the insurance.' She sobbed. 'I'm going to lose my job because the shop is going to close, and I'm going to jail.'

'Did you know or participate in this?' Emma placed the pile of invoices in the black tray, leaving one on the desk.

'No, but I know now.' Noelle wiped the tears from her cheeks. 'I'm so screwed. Who's going to hire me after this? My reputation is ruined.'

Emma narrowed her eyes. 'Noelle, how old are you? Not the age on your résumé. Your real age.'

Noelle hung her head. 'On my résumé, I said that I was twenty-two. But I'm almost seventeen. I moved out of my mum's house the day I turned sixteen. My mother's boyfriend is an idiot. And they have a new baby. They've replaced me.'

'I'm sorry about that.' Emma sighed. 'But you don't have any criminal liability because you're just an employee. You didn't know. But what about your job with the poster boy next door? You could ask for more hours. He seems to be all alone at the Berry Crumb.'

Noelle smiled as she dried her eyes. 'Oh yeah. I forgot about the Berry Crumb. And I have an Artsy store where I sell crochet patterns.'

Emma raised her eyebrows. 'You have three jobs.'

Standing, Emma turned then walked up the length of the

stockroom. As she reached the door, she paused, pulled out her smartphone, and tapped the screen.

'I'm coming with you.' Noelle scurried after Emma as she opened the door and disappeared into the shop.

———

A loud *creak* echoed through the shop. Emma grimaced then paused as she listened to the whispering subside. So much for a surprise entrance. If she had known the shop floor a little better, she would've known how to avoid the floorboard. She gestured at Noelle, who was behind her. Hopefully, the teenager wouldn't follow her to the counter.

'Noelle,' Elsie called out, 'you don't have to stay behind. I'll finish the stocktake on my own.'

Emma waved her finger as Noelle opened her mouth. 'Don't come out of the bookshelves for anything. Go back to the security cameras,' she whispered.

Noelle shook her head. Of course she wanted to stay on the shop floor with the felons.

Emma stepped out from the safety of the bookshelves. 'It's just me.'

All the blood drained from Elsie's face. The shopkeeper looked like a deer caught in headlights. Emma peered at George, who had turned around and propped against the counter as if waiting for a pint at the local pub. In one swift movement, Elsie grabbed the insurance documents and slipped them under the counter. That could mean only one thing—someone was committing insurance fraud after all and not getting started on the papers.

Emma smiled. 'Lord Harrington, I didn't realise you collected rent in person. That's a little old-fashioned.'

George chuckled. 'No.' He waved dismissively. 'I like to

visit all of my commercial properties, especially my favourite ones.' He smiled.

'Silly me. Here I was thinking your frequent visits to the shop were to pressure Elsie to come up with the rent for her shop space and even convince her to commit insurance fraud.' Emma shrugged. 'It must be that wild imagination of mine getting the better of me. So I guess this means you're just here to forge the *Gatsby* on that working printing press at the back of your antique shop.'

George's eyes widened as he turned and dashed towards the front doors. He turned the handle and shook the doors, but they were fastened shut. When Elsie had locked the door earlier, he must not have been paying attention. He simply jabbered on, blissfully unaware that he was trapped.

'I can explain.' Elsie collapsed into the chair. 'I've been paying the rent from my savings, and I'm so desperate that I thought if the book was stolen, I could claim it back on insurance.'

George gasped. 'You've dragged my good name into the mud.'

'Oh, so you draw the line at insurance fraud.' Emma raised her eyebrows. 'It's good to see you have standards.'

'Now, hear me, missy—'

'Emma, Lord Harrington had nothing to do with the stolen *Gatsby*.' Tears streamed down Elsie's cheeks.

Lord Harrington straightened; he was like a petulant child with chocolate smeared all over his face, swearing he didn't have a cookie.

'I know the theft of the *Gatsby* was staged.' Emma shook her head. 'I've figured it out. You're welcome to stick to your story, but you've been caught.'

'You don't know what it's like to have a dream slip through your fingers like this. If you were in my position, you would do the same thing.' Elsie glanced at the bookshelves running along the wall behind the checkout counter.

'Actually, I do know what this is like. And I didn't stoop to criminal activity to protect something I created in my mother's attic when I was eighteen.' Emma sighed. 'That's why I offered to help you. I lost Byte Tech to my soon-to-be ex-husband and that boys' club that he dares to call a board. I thought you were like me.'

'Ladies, ladies.' George held up his hands. 'There's a simple solution to all of this. I'll buy the *Gatsby*, and no one will have to commit insurance fraud.'

So, he wasn't even attempting to deny the forgery—that was interesting.

Emma froze as the faint sound of sirens cried out in the background. So the triple-nine operator, who had been on the line via the smartphone in the back pocket of her jeans, had heard the conversation and sent the police.

Elsie jumped up from the armchair behind the counter then whirled around and faced George. 'You were never going to buy the *Gatsby*. Emma's right. You're just working on another forgery.'

That was why Victoria had been in Turning Pages earlier that morning. She'd gotten a signed paperback from Charles Thomas Worthington III and was checking out the signatures in Elsie's shop. Victoria was onto him, which meant the novel Emma had purchased from Leaf & Leather probably had a fraudulent signature too. Perfect.

'Let me out.' George slammed his fist on the front door. 'I don't have to take any more of this nonsense from either of you.'

Elsie scowled. 'In your dreams.'

Emma rolled her eyes. 'You can't keep him here. Let him out.'

She glared at Emma.

'Let him out,' Emma snapped.

The tall, thin, pink-haired woman sauntered around the counter then across the room and unlocked the door. She turned and held the door open for George. Before he could leave, two police cars drove up, slammed on their brakes, and brought their cars to a screeching halt, blocking the narrow hedge-lined laneway of Berry Drive.

## TURNING THE PAGE

Through the Old Mill House Tavern's bay window, shadows gathered along the dimly lit street. Outside, the streetlight flickered as Noelle climbed into a taxi and waved at Emma through the window. Frost formed on the edge of the bay window as the outside temperature dropped. The deep charcoal-grey sky was covered with winter clouds that obscured the twinkling stars and hung over the sleeping village of Saint James Upon Berry.

Inside, the tavern bustled with chatter from the locals—not just pensioners as she'd expected but young families, teenagers, and plenty of patrons barely older than herself. Maybe they had left the city and moved out there for a quieter life for their children. Cradled in her hands was another dainty blue-and-white teacup with that vintage blue Asiatic pheasants pattern, and on the table sat a matching teapot filled with chamomile tea.

The events of the evening played through her mind like scenes from a movie: George being guided towards the police car for further questioning at the police station in Little Oak, Elsie breaking down and confessing to the insurance fraud scheme, and Noelle insisting that she wouldn't talk to the police without Emma present. The teenager must have been terrified that the police would call her parents, but quite surprisingly, they were okay with those terms.

But what puzzled Emma the most was Elsie's emotional breakdown and confession. It was as if she'd wanted to get arrested. Thanks to her actions, she would face a custodial sentence of up to four years but more likely to be reduced to nine months because of the attempted insurance fraud.

A couple of hours after the arrest, while Emma was making a formal statement at the station, she overheard the police chatting. After securing a last-minute warrant by calling a nearby judge at his home, the police searched the workshop behind Harrington & Co. Fine Antiquities. They discovered an unfinished forgery of the first edition *Gatsby* and a pile of paperbacks signed by Charles Thomas Worthington III, which one officer referred to as suspicious.

The officers were beyond excited by George's printing press and piles of paper with practice attempts at forging the signatures of other famous authors. They chatted animatedly about how the printing press was beautifully restored and in working order. After overhearing that news, Emma surrendered the seven-hundred-and-fifty-pounds signed paperback she'd purchased from Leaf & Leather. The officer glanced at the signature on the title page of her copy of Last Night by Charles Thomas Worthington III and said the signature wasn't authentic. So that was seven hundred and fifty pounds flushed down the drain.

But that wasn't the only thing she overheard. During a search of the crime scene, the police had discovered the closed-off stairwell with the hidden ladder that led to the first floor above the shop. Poor Elsie had been sleeping on the floor in the commercial space above Turning Pages. It was heartbreaking to hear, and Emma teared up as she listened to the police officers retelling the story.

The bank had repossessed Elsie's house because she couldn't afford the mortgage. She must have struggled to pay for both her house and the shop. That explained the maze-like setup in Turning Pages—it wasn't just creative merchandising but a way to maximise space when she could no longer afford the utility bills for the ground and first floors. It must have been freezing up there in the winter, especially if she hadn't opened the valves of the gas radiators.

According to evidence discovered in the black trays in the stockroom, her house had been repossessed six months ago, and the stairs to the upper level were removed around the same time. She was also in arrears with her gas, water, and electricity bills for the shop. But that wasn't the only thing they found in the stockroom. At the back of the bottom drawer in the desk, wrapped in fabric, was the *Gatsby*—it had never left the shop.

Desperate didn't begin to describe Elsie's situation. But worst of all, her desperate attempts to save her shop would be the reason her shop would close for good.

Emma took another sip of tea then cradled the teacup in her hand as she gazed at the cloudy night sky. Far off in the background, the brass bell above the tavern's door jangled as another person entered. Footfall pattered across the oak flooring and past the bar, heading for the seating area.

'I'm pretty sure you're supposed to hold that by the handle.' Ben chuckled as he sat down next to her.

She raised her eyebrows at him.

'What?' He winked. 'Is this seat reserved or something?'

Emma leaned to the side as she turned and peered up at him. 'Did you just wink at me?'

Ben threw his hands in the air. 'Sorry. I can't help it. It's a bad habit. Sometimes, I can't turn it off.'

'Oh, really?'

Ben smiled. 'Should I set aside a baguette for you tomorrow?' Ben stood then turned around. 'You know how hangry you get if you don't eat.'

Emma rolled her eyes then took another sip of her tea. She wasn't going to dignify that last comment with a response.

As she refocused on the sleepy village that lay outside the bay window, she smiled. Part of her didn't want to leave. In all of the drama of the theatrical-style theft and eventual arrests, Emma had missed a call from a young man called Toby, who didn't sound old enough to run a business, saying that he would stop by her cottage at half eleven in the morning to fix the upstairs radiator. On top of that, she still hadn't purchased a book for her mother.

Then it dawned on her. For the first time in quite a while, Emma felt like she belonged somewhere. Instead of renting out her cottage, she could do minor renovations and trade in the city life for stress-free living in Saint James Upon Berry.

# Glossary of British Slang

**Cheeky:** *adjective.* a little bit naughty but nice
**Chinwag:** *noun.* a chat
**Codswallop:** *noun.* nonsense
**Dodgy:** *noun.* risky, difficult, or dangerous
**Faff:** *verb.* make a fuss over something trivial or to mess around and take too much time to achieve nothing
**High Street:** The main street in a town, city, or village where most of the shops and businesses are located, which is also common used as a metonym for the retail sector.
**Knackered:** *noun.* exhausted
**Quid:** *noun.* one pound sterling
**Rubbish:** *noun.* nonsense
**So-and-so:** *noun.* a person regarded as unpleasant or difficult

# Also by Amelia D. Hay

### Emma Warwick Mystery Series

Step into the charming English village of St James Upon Berry, where former tech CEO Emma Warwick trades London's fast pace for country living. But small-village life isn't quite as peaceful as she imagined.

### A Fatal Steeping (Prequel Short Story)

A stormy afternoon at Bath's Georgian Leaf Tearoom turns deadly when a regular patron is poisoned. Trapped by the power outage with an eclectic group of suspects, tech CEO Emma Warwick must solve the crime by candlelight. But in this historic tearoom, everyone has something to hide.

### A First Edition Felony (Book 1)

A rare first edition of The Great Gatsby has vanished from a village bookshop, and former tech CEO Emma Warwick is the only one who suspects foul play. Armed with her business savvy and tech expertise, she's determined to uncover the truth behind the seemingly perfect crime.

### A Will to Murder (Book 2) - Coming Soon

When a crime writer dies, the real story begins… Tech executive Emma Warwick trades London for village life, but she doesn't expect to inherit a murder mystery. With her elderly neighbour Dotty by her side, she'll discover that in Hampshire, even a quiet memorial service can hide deadly secrets.

# Get a Free Cozy Mystery Short Story

One teacup, one storm, one murder. Afternoon tea will never be the same.

Emma Warwick planned to nurse her heartbreak with green rose tea and polite conversation at the Georgian Leaf Tearoom in Bath. But when a beloved local drops dead over a cup of Earl Grey, Emma finds herself steeped in scandal, secrets, and a suspiciously silent sugar bowl.

Trapped by a raging storm with a room full of strangers, and at least one murderer, Emma must rely on her sharp instincts and boardroom-honed wit to untangle a web of lies.

But the more she digs, the more she realises someone in the tearoom has everything to lose.

In a world where heritage meets homicide, can a freshly

betrayed tech executive solve a murder before the killer strikes again?

———

If you love a page turning cozy mystery, you can get the ebook for A Fatal Steeping for free now: ameliadhay.com/free-book/

# Thank You

While writing a book is a solitary pursuit, creating a book is a collaborative effort. A First Edition Felony marks the beginning of Emma Warwick's adventures in Saint James Upon Berry, and I have many people to thank for helping bring this literary world to life.

Firstly, a special thank you goes out to my alpha reader, Eric, whom I stumbled across on Fiverr, of all places, for your knowledge and witty comments on my revised draft. Eric, you helped me create a more realistic story, and your input was, once again, invaluable. Especially your comments and knowledge of electric vehicles helped this non-driver add another level of realism to the story.

To my beta readers, Cait Lynn and Madelyn, thank you for reading and loving my books and for your comments, which helped me shape my story.

One of the most challenging parts of the publishing process was the three rounds of line edits I decided to embark upon two days after Christmas. Yes, you read that correctly. You live and learn. So, a massive thank you goes to my long-suffering line editor, Angela. Thank you for putting up with me.

And to my proofreader, Brittany thank you for the last minute tidbits you added during this final stage of editing—these comments helped me take my book to the next level.

Finally, to my readers—thank you for joining Emma on her first adventure. I hope you enjoy exploring Saint James Upon Berry as much as I enjoyed creating it.

With love,

Amelia xx

# A Note From the Author

Thank you for reading *A First Edition Felony*, the first instalment in the Emma Warwick Mystery series. This story holds a special place in my heart as it marks the beginning of Emma's journey from tech CEO to amateur sleuth. When I first created Emma, her last name was Scott, which I changed later after discovering an author with the same name. I set out to create a character who was a little like me approaching or a little past her forties that other people my age might relate to, but that's where the similarities end.

A simple writing prompt planted the seed for this story: 'Rare books start disappearing from a quaint bookshop.' What began as an exercise in crafting a short story to use as a back-of-the-book freebie for people who read *A Will to Murder* quickly took on a life of its own. The original target was a concise 10,000 words, but Emma and the residents of Saint James Upon Berry had other plans. As the story unfolded and the characters came to life, the word count grew past 19,000 words, transforming a short story into a novella. In light of this increased word count, *A First Edition*

*Felony* became book one in the series, and *A Will to Murder* became book two.

The setting of Saint James Upon Berry was inspired by my research into the filming locations of ITV's Miss Marple series. I ended up falling down a rabbit hole when the picturesque English villages featured in the show captured my imagination, and I found myself wanting to create a similar sense of timeless charm and mystery. These locations helped shape the world where Emma would begin her new life and discover her talent for solving mysteries. Unfortunately, it's not a real-life location.

In crafting Emma's character, I wanted to explore how someone might reinvent themselves after betrayal while holding onto their core strengths. Emma's tech background gives her a unique perspective on problem-solving, which proves invaluable in her new role as an amateur detective. The technological elements in the story, from the security cameras to Emma's electric car, provide an interesting contrast to the traditional cozy mystery setting.

Just between you and me, the affair between Stephen St Clair and the unnamed head of HR was inspired by a real-life scandal in a famous tech company—this scandal made it to the news. And it was too good not to be included in this story.

The characters of the Turning Pages bookshop—Elsie, Noelle, and even Lord Harrington—each brought their own surprises during the writing process. What started as a simple case of a missing book evolved into a complex web of relationships, secrets, and unexpected connections that would affect Emma's future adventures.

*A First Edition Felony* sets the stage for the events in *A Will to Murder* and provides an essential context for Emma's character development. We see her at her most vulnerable, yet this vulnerability ultimately leads her to discover her new passion for solving mysteries.

I hope you enjoyed your visit to Saint James Upon Berry. Emma's journey is just beginning, and I look forward to sharing more of her adventures with you.

With love,

*Amelia xx*

———

**P.S.** For those wondering about Emma's designer shopping spree on her soon-to-be ex-husband's credit card—sometimes the best revenge is charged in monthly instalments.

# About the Author

Amelia D. Hay writes cozy mysteries set in the charming English village of Saint James Upon Berry, where bookshops hide secrets and historic properties harbour mysteries waiting to be solved. Her Emma Warwick Mystery series combines classic British mystery traditions with contemporary wit and warmth. It features an amateur sleuth who trades London's tech world for village life, only to find herself untangling suspicious deaths and missing treasures.

When she is not crafting intricate mysteries, Amelia explores European cities, drinks copious amounts of tea, and indulges in pizza.

Originally from Brisbane, Australia, Amelia now lives in London, where she finds endless inspiration in the city's literary history and quaint villages beyond the metropolis.

To learn more about Amelia's books, or to join her author newsletter to receive updates on new releases at:
ameliadhay.com

amazon.com/stores/Amelia-D.-Hay/author/B0DTV338LS

bsky.app/profile/authorameliadhay.bsky.social

bookbub.com/authors/amelia-d-hay

facebook.com/ameliadhaywrites

goodreads.com/ameliadhaywrites

instagram.com/ameliadhaywrites

threads.com/@ameliadhaywrites